“Who ca

e man who led nst the English king? Ms. sked.

No one volunteered an answer.

Sighing, Ms. Chalmers walked over to the light switch, then raised a remote control and turned on a TV and VCR sitting on a cart in the corner. “Perhaps this will refresh your memories.”

As the room darkened and a battle sequence from a movie appeared on the screen, Sabrina crossed her fingers. She didn’t pop.

“Oh, I know!” Jill, cheerleader and one of Libby’s faithful companions, called out. “Mel Gibson!”

A wave of laughter rippled through the room.

Harvey whispered, “William Wallace in *Braveheart.*”

“Yes, I know.” Sabrina glanced over her shoulder—

Pinggggg!

—and saw thousands of crudely dressed men and boys covering the grassy hill behind her. Carrying leather shields, swords, axes, wooden spears, and farm implements, they stood ready to fight and die for Scotland and the courageous man riding on the plain before them.

Looking up, she saw Wallace and the nobles riding back from the failed negotiations with the English army. The battle was going to start any minute.

“Why couldn’t I have popped into one of the romantic scenes in the beginning?” she moaned.

A hundred archers assembled in front of the king’s mounted knights. . . .

Sabrina, the Teenage Witch™ books

#1 Sabrina, the Teenage Witch
#2 Showdown at the Mall
#3 Good Switch, Bad Switch
#4 Halloween Havoc
#5 Santa's Little Helper
#6 Ben There, Done That
#7 All You Need Is a Love Spell
#8 Salem on Trial
#9 A Dog's Life
#10 Lotsa Luck
#11 Prisoner of Cabin 13
#12 All That Glitters
#13 Go Fetch!
#14 Spying Eyes
Sabrina Goes to Rome
#15 Harvest Moon
#16 Now You See Her, Now You Don't

Available from ARCHWAY Paperbacks

Now You See Her, Now You Don't

Diana G. Gallagher

Based on Characters Appearing in Archie Comics

And based upon the television series
Sabrina, The Teenage Witch
Created for television by Nell Scovell
Developed for television by Jonathan Schmock

AN ARCHWAY PAPERBACK
Published by POCKET BOOKS
New York London Toronto Sydney Tokyo Singapore

AN ARCHWAY PAPERBACK *Original*

An Archway Paperback published by
POCKET BOOKS, a division of Simon & Schuster Inc.
1230 Avenue of the Americas, New York, NY 10020

ISBN: 0-671-02120-6

First Archway Paperback printing December 1998

10 9 8 7 6 5 4 3 2 1

Printed in the U.S.A.

IL: 4+

With affection
for Jennifer Alyse Carter,
friend and future author

Now You See Her, Now You Don't

☆

Chapter 1

☆

Throwing back the covers, Sabrina sprang out of bed, spread her arms, and burst into song. "Oh, what a beautiful morning. Oh, what a beautiful day. I've got—"

"I'm awake! I'm awake!" Salem leaped to his feet on the end of the bed and did a double take when he realized Sabrina, and not the radio alarm, was responsible for his rude awakening. "My! Aren't *you* just so perky today. What's the occasion?"

"Nothing. In fact, everything's terrific. It's Friday and I finished my English term paper last night." Sabrina smiled. "And it's not due until Monday."

"Congratulations. I hereby decree that you're no

longer eligible for membership in Procrastinators Anonymous." Yawning, Salem eyed her narrowly. "You're not feeling feverish, are you?"

"No. I feel great! Why?"

"Aside from the fact that you're suspiciously cheerful for a teenager who just woke up on a school day and you're suddenly prone to spontaneous musical seizures, it's *not* a beautiful day." Craning his neck, Salem stared out the window. "The mercury may soar to all of fifteen by noon and there's a blizzard sweeping down from Canada."

"It's still a beautiful day," Sabrina insisted.

Worried, Salem frowned. "Get the book."

"What for?"

"You've obviously come down with an acute case of Pollyanna Plague. There's no time to waste."

"Pollyanna Plague?" Sabrina raised an eyebrow. "Isn't Pollyanna a character in a book?"

"Yes. Written by Eleanor H. Porter about a sweet orphaned girl who's *always* happy! Yuck."

Sabrina laughed.

"See!" Salem sat back with a gasp. "You've got all the symptoms. Victims suffer from irrational fits of giddiness, uncontrollable smiling, and extreme optimism in the face of dire disaster. And it's highly contagious. We've got to find the cure, and quick!"

"I'm not sick." Grinning impishly, Sabrina jumped onto the chair by the window and belted out the rest of the Rodgers and Hammerstein lyric. "I've got a wonderful feeling everything's going my way!"

"Oh, no. We're all going to spend a miserable weekend being euphoric and hooked on glad games. I think I'm gonna be sick." Salem gagged. "To my stomach."

"Not on the bed, please."

"Chill. Apparently, my throat is fur-ball free." Sighing, Salem hung his head.

"Well, that's something to be glad about, isn't it?"

"No," Salem snapped. "Not when I want to make a symbolic statement of disgust."

"Come on, Salem." Perching on the edge of the bed, Sabrina stopped smiling. "I've got good reasons to be happy this morning."

"Yeah? Like what?"

"Like I passed one of the Quizmaster's surprise tests yesterday afternoon." Pointing at the closet, Sabrina opened the doors. Hangers slid along the bar as she searched for something to wear. "So I don't have to worry about him springing another pop quiz on me all weekend."

"Unless *he's* feeling more Quizmasterish than usual." Salem looked up. "I mean, you expect surprise tests after a certain amount of time has passed, right?"

"Yeah. What's your point?"

"If you *expect* something, it's not a surprise. But

springing *another* pop quiz on you right after you just had one *would* be a surprise." Salem peered at Sabrina intently.

"He wouldn't." Sabrina dropped the jeans and turtleneck she had chosen and frowned uncertainly. "Would he?"

Salem shrugged.

"Naw. He won't," Sabrina said confidently. "He's spending the weekend at one of those sulfuric hot spring dome resorts on Venus."

"That ranks right up there with toad sucking and bungee jumping off the Eiffel Tower. Not on *my* list of want-to-dos."

"Not too high on mine, either. There are so many better ways to spend a free weekend." Sabrina lifted the fallen outfit and tossed it on her chair with a flamboyant flick of her finger.

"Such as?" Salem asked.

"For starters, going to the roller rink with Harvey tonight."

"Now that gets a lukewarm whoop-de-do from me."

Refusing to let Salem bring her down, Sabrina grabbed her robe and headed down the hall. Most school days she overslept and had to zap herself clean, which wasn't nearly as invigorating as taking a real shower in the morning.

But she wasn't going to get one today either. Clad in a "Witchfest '76" T-shirt and rumpled gray sweatpants, Aunt Hilda was planted in front of the bathroom mirror, scowling at her reflection.

"Is something wrong, Aunt Hilda?"

"Yes! All these little, tiny wrinkles around my eyes! My face has been sabotaged." Leaning closer to the mirror, Aunt Hilda winced.

"By time or treachery?" Sabrina asked lightly.

"Good question." Aunt Hilda shot her niece a suspicious glance. "You didn't accidentally dump any Crow's Feet Crone Flakes into the raisin bran, did you?"

"No. In fact, I just passed a magic pop quiz on identifying basic spell ingredients by smell, texture, and appearance. Crone Flakes aren't as crispy as bran flakes."

"Then I really *am* aging prematurely."

Sabrina diplomatically didn't mention that Aunt Hilda was over six hundred years old. While the aging process took a lot longer, witches did grow old just like mortals.

"There must be an anti-aging potion or a wrinkle-removing spell you can use?" The youth candy she had whipped up on Aunt Zelda's labtop to help her vice-principal recall what it was like to be a teenager wasn't an option. The spell worked on the mind, not the body, and the consequences were disastrous if the candy was mixed with caffeine. Mr. Kraft's iced-tea pitcher had absorbed the potion and continued to dispense it. The school, Aunt Hilda, and the vice-principal had barely survived his steady regression into a kindergarten mentality.

"Nothing that works." Sighing, Aunt Hilda sank onto the commode. "Cleopatra's court magicians came close to developing an anti-aging formula, but they gave up after a hundred volunteers had their faces turn to stone."

"But it can't be *that* hard to smooth out a few little wrinkles."

"No, it's not. But most people would rather have wrinkles than green scales."

Sabrina grimaced.

"Witches have been trying to break the age barrier for millennia without much success. Then again—" Aunt Hilda brightened suddenly. "Zelda is infinitely more brilliant than the others who have tried . . ."

"Oh, is that why she's been gallivanting around Europe the past few days?" Aunt Zelda took pride in her appearance but had a level head when it came to accepting certain facts of life that couldn't be changed. Like getting old several centuries down the road.

"I begged her." Hilda shrugged sheepishly. "The medieval alchemists weren't totally focused on turning lead into gold, you know. They spent most of their time looking for the elixir of perpetual youth. Zelda's been scouring museums and library archives looking for their notes."

"Did she find anything?"

"I think so. She mumbled something about finding a basic youth formula or a recipe for fruitcake when she finally popped home last night."

"So there's hope!"

Aunt Hilda sighed. "Not if Zelda's confidence level stays bottomed out at zero. She keeps insisting that there are some things the 'chemistry of magic' can't cure." Hilda turned back to the mirror.

Having spent her shower time talking, Sabrina rushed back down the hall to zap herself ready for school. Her best friend, Val, was meeting her before first period to review the questions for a teen poll they were conducting at lunch. If their "Students Speak" column was a hit in next week's edition of the *Westbridge Lantern,* Val was going to run it as a regular feature.

It was promising to be a perfect day.

"How can you take a shower and not get your hair wet?" Sitting on the wicker laundry basket outside the linen closet, Salem licked a paw and continued grooming himself.

Sabrina paused in the bedroom doorway. "Hilda's on wrinkle watch in the bathroom and I'm not doing depression today."

"You're just looking for trouble, aren't you?" Salem shook his head. "Don't you know that feeling great is like sending an open invitation for disaster to strike!"

"Stop fretting, Salem! I've got everything in my life under control for a change. What could possibly go wrong?"

Lightning flashed in the linen closet.

"I wonder who that could be?" Salem's voice oozed sarcasm. "Disaster calling!"

Disaster didn't even begin to describe the peril emerging from the Other Realm. Sabrina jumped back as the linen closet door flew open.

Amanda!

☆

Chapter 2

☆

Ducking behind the bedroom door as her malevolent little cousin stormed out of the closet, Sabrina stubbed her toe. Clenching her teeth, she endured the pain in silence and hoped the girl hadn't noticed her.

What in Drell's name was the scourge of the Spellman family doing here?

Freshly bathed and smelling of lavender soap, Amanda was the image of sweet girlish charm in a long-sleeved, forest green velvet dress with white lace trim draped over layers of crisp crinolines. But in her case, appearances were decidedly deceiving. Long dark curls framed a porcelain doll face cast in a perpetual petulant scowl.

Sabrina didn't have time to defend herself against Amanda's annoying spells. However, since she could be showered and dressed with a quick point and pop herself to school, avoiding Amanda wasn't a problem.

Salem was fair game for the ruthless brat, though.

"Uh-oh." Caught in the open by the one-girl terror brigade, Salem tried to sound the alarm. "Wicked witch on deck—"

Sabrina chanced a peek as Amanda pointed.

"Look at that! A ceramic cat!" The small witch sneered as feline bone, muscle, and fur became a glazed black cookie jar with a Cheshire-cat smile and large, plastic-toy eyes that blinked in surprise.

Sagging behind her bedroom door, Sabrina sighed. Rushed or not, she had to rescue the cat.

And hope Amanda wasn't in the mood to challenge her.

She really didn't want to miss the meeting with Val. Dedicated to social advancement at any cost, Val would be devastated if anything happened to ruin her shot at editorial and journalistic fame, her passport to in-crowd acceptance.

And where Amanda was concerned, anything could happen.

Such as being turned into a doll and trapped in a toy box. Sabrina's wits had saved her and Amanda's other prisoners that time, but she couldn't afford any unnecessary delay right now.

Engaging her magic finger, Sabrina dressed in a

black turtleneck, yellow jeans, and her low-cut black boots, then pointed her school bag and books into her arms. She opened the door just as Amanda marched down the hall. Salem the cookie jar disappeared with a casual flick of the girl's hand.

Incensed, Sabrina started to shout when Aunt Hilda barged out of the bathroom. She swallowed the protest when Amanda stopped at the head of the stairs. Letting her more experienced aunt deal with the tiny tyrant seemed like a much better idea than getting personally involved. At least, Amanda would think twice before trying any mischievous whammies on Aunt Hilda, an edge Sabrina didn't have.

"Zelda!" Aunt Hilda shouted toward her sister's closed bedroom door. Facing the opposite end of the hall, she couldn't see Cousin Marigold's delinquent daughter behind her.

Intent on Aunt Hilda, Amanda didn't realize Sabrina was standing behind her.

"How can you sleep while I'm turning into a wrinkled prune? Get up and get busy! I've got a date with Willard tonight!"

No response.

Stepping back into the doorway, Sabrina used her finger to scribble a note on the bathroom mirror where Hilda was sure to see it. Once her aunts knew what Amanda had done to Salem, they'd make her undo it—or else.

"Your face isn't permanent-press either, Zelda!"

Amanda giggled.

Hilda stiffened, then whirled. "What are you doing here?"

"Those aren't wrinkles." Ignoring Hilda's question, Amanda pointed. *"These* are wrinkles!"

Hilda's facial skin sagged suddenly. Drooping folds of loose skin re-formed into dozens of sharpei wrinkles with a disgusting sucking sound.

Fascinated, Sabrina stopped writing to stare. Furious and focused on Amanda, Aunt Hilda didn't notice her, either.

"Reverse that spell this instant, Amanda, or I'll feed you to the cat."

"Salem can't hurt me!" Crossing her arms, Amanda lifted her chin in stubborn defiance.

"Not our cat." Hilda pointed toward her bedroom.

A lion roared and smashed through the closed door with unsheathed claws.

"That cat."

Pouting, Amanda pointed again and Aunt Hilda's face returned to normal.

Sabrina finished her note about Salem.

"I don't know what you're doing here, Amanda, but you weren't invited." Glaring, Hilda wagged her finger in the little witch's face.

"So?"

Rolling her eyes, knowing her aunts were in for a long day with the bratty little girl, Sabrina leaned forward to check her reflection in the mirror at the end of the hall opposite Aunt Hilda. *Perfect! I'm out of here.*

"So—" Fuming, Hilda chanted:

"Witches pop in and out in books and TV,
But you can't pop in here whenever you please!"

Hilda's wagging finger snapped toward the little witch.

Amanda ducked.

Pointing on a gray parka with white fake-fur trim and matching mittens, Sabrina popped to school.

Dizzy, with an odd *pinging* sound in her ears, Sabrina didn't realize for a moment that she wasn't in school. She was standing by the front porch of a Victorian house that was larger and more ornate than the Spellman residence. Birds sang in the leafy giant oaks dotting the rolling lawn, and bees buzzed around perfectly tended flower gardens.

"Hi!" a young voice said brightly.

Turning around, Sabrina stared at a girl with long blond braids sitting in a porch swing. The braids were tied with huge powder blue bows that matched a mid-calf-length blue-and-white checked dress. Ankle boots and frilly pantaloons completed the country ensemble. Still wearing a parka guaranteed to keep her warm at subzero temperatures, Sabrina started to sweat under the sizzling summer sun.

"You look worried. And hot." The girl reached

for a pitcher of lemonade on a wicker table beside the swing. "Would you like a cool drink?"

"Uh—no. Thanks." Sabrina's mind raced. Her popping power was obviously malfunctioning, but she hadn't made any charms, mixed any potions, or cast any spells beyond routine pointing in the past couple of days. She was absolutely certain she hadn't done anything magical that could possibly backfire.

"Are you here to see my aunt?" The girl asked in a lilting, innocent voice that sounded sincere.

"No. Wherever this is, I'm not supposed to be here."

"Where are you supposed to be?"

"Westbridge High School."

"Well, you're not at school!" Laughing merrily, the girl pushed against the porch with her feet to start the swing swinging. "And that's something to be glad about!"

"Glad?"

"Oh, yes." The girl nodded emphatically. "Whenever anything bad happens, I can always find *something* to be glad about."

Sabrina's eyes widened. "Who are—"

"Pollyanna!" A sharp voice shouted inside the house. "Don't you dare get dirty! The reverend will be here for tea any minute!"

"The maid really shouldn't fret so. Nervous conditions can be so difficult." Pollyanna sighed. "I think being happy can cure vapors and melancholy, but no one believes me."

Groaning, Sabrina touched her forehead. Her skin *did* feel hot, but she couldn't tell if that was because she had a fever or because she was bundled up enough to survive an arctic winter. However, she suspected Salem was right—she must have an acute case of Pollyanna Plague.

More like Bucolic Plague, she thought, with a sweeping glance at the rustic surroundings.

The driver of a horse-drawn buggy breezing down the road tipped his hat to a woman strolling on the sidewalk with a parasol. Two boys wearing knickers rolled a metal hoop with a stick down the quaint street.

"You see, having tea with the reverend and Aunt Polly could give me a sour stomach." Whispering, Pollyanna grimaced, then grinned again. "But it's the only time I get to eat those fancy little sugar cookies with cherries on top that Cook bakes, so my stomach behaves. And I'm *very* glad about that!"

Sabrina blinked—

Ping!

—and staggered as she popped into the restroom near her locker. Dizzy, she leaned against the sink and wondered if hallucinating was another symptom of the plague Salem had neglected to mention.

Hilda sagged with relief when her little cousin Amanda vanished from the hall, then turned and raised her fist to pound on Zelda's door. She almost pounded on Zelda's head when the door suddenly opened.

"What is going on out here, Hilda?" Bleary-eyed and disheveled, Zelda pulled her robe closed and tied the sash.

"I'm turning into a withered old hag."

"Besides that. I thought I heard giggling."

"You did." Wrinkling her nose to explain, Hilda jumped when the linen closet boomed and lit up to announce an impending arrival from the Other Realm. She exhaled with relief when Cousin Marigold limped out wearing one high heel and carrying the other.

"Where is she?" Grabbing the doorknob to steady herself, Marigold slipped on her other shoe. Straightening, she tugged at the bottom of a white linen jacket, then pushed a loose hairpin back into her perfect French twist.

No one should look that flawlessly elegant so early in the day, Hilda mused. She restrained the urge to point herself into less frumpy attire.

"Where is who, Marigold?" Zelda asked.

"Amanda!"

"Don't worry. I just sent her back to the Other Realm." Hilda faltered. "I think."

"You *think?*" Marigold and Zelda asked in alarmed unison.

"No, I'm sure." Hilda's voice sounded more certain than she actually felt. "For a split second, though, I thought my spell missed her."

Which, Hilda thought, *would have been catastrophic.* The Other Realm was protected by wards that absorbed and nullified the chaotic, destructive effects of a child's magical tantrums. The mortal world, on the other hand, was defenseless.

"Do you have any idea how much damage Amanda can do if she's running loose in this realm, Hilda?" Appalled, Zelda threw up her arms. "I mean, there's only so much that pointing can fix!"

"I know, I know." Hilda waved her sister's concerns aside. It wasn't likely that the government would provide disaster relief for victims of a witch's foul mood, either, but that, like the discussion, was irrelevant. "Relax. Amanda vanished, so my spell must have worked. She's probably back in her room plotting revenge."

"As long as she's not here." Marigold wilted with relief. "Amanda can be so unruly when she gets in a snit and I don't have time to clean up after her right now."

"You do have an amazing flair for understatement, Marigold." Running her hand through her tangled hair, Zelda glared at Hilda. "Having an unguided spell ricocheting all over the place looking for a target wouldn't have been a party, either. Especially for whoever it locked onto and zapped."

"Ricochet spells don't always have the intended effect, either," Marigold added. "They get distorted."

Hilda was well aware of that. When they were children, Zelda had cast a spell to clean and press a gown. The garment had fallen off the chair at the exact same instant. The spell had ricocheted off a reflective silver medallion on the castle wall and hit her. She had been "pressed" to clean everything without pause for two days before Zelda had taken pity on her and reversed it. Getting the entire medieval castle to gleam like the tower room they shared would have taken her ten years.

Hilda changed the subject before Zelda settled into lecture mode. "What was Amanda doing here anyway, Marigold?"

"Running away from home." Rubbing her temples, Marigold winced. "I don't suppose you've got a cup of coffee?"

Zelda nodded wearily. "I could use one myself."

Hilda smiled. "I'll brew, Zelda. You need to be wide-awake before you get to work."

Sitting cross-legged on the bed, Amanda grinned. Adults could be so annoying, but they weren't going to spoil her fun this time.

She had no idea what had happened to Hilda's spell, but it certainly hadn't zapped her! She had ducked to avoid it, then popped out of the hall of her own free will so Hilda would *think* the spell had worked.

Nobody knew what had really happened to her.

Because she hadn't popped back to her own room or anywhere else in the Other Realm.

She was in Sabrina's room.

Which was badly in need of redecorating.

For starters.

Chapter 3

"There you are!"

Sabrina jumped as Val burst through the restroom door. One minute sooner and the girl would have found her totally zoned out, present in body but mentally absent.

"Sabrina? Are you okay?"

"Uh, yeah."

"Are you sure? You look a little pale."

Sabrina thought about that as she slipped off her parka. Now that the weird pinging and dizziness had passed, she felt fine. In fact, she still felt great. Her English term paper was done, the Quizmaster was on vacation, and unless something unexpected had come up, Harvey was going roller-skating with her that night. She had even escaped a potentially disastrous encounter with Amanda.

"Please don't tell me you're sick." A stricken look flashed across Val's face. "I can't do the 'Students Speak' survey by myself. I get tongue-tied when I'm nervous, and public speaking makes me very nervous."

"Asking a bunch of kids a question in the cafeteria doesn't really qualify as public speaking, Val."

"Maybe not, but Libby will be watching. She's just waiting for me to foul up so Mrs. Quick will make her editor of the *Lantern.*" Val stiffened, her eyes widening. "Omigod! What if I get the giggles? Or motor-mouth? Or worse! Verbal dyslexia! I would lotally kreaf!"

" 'Lotally kreaf'?" Sabrina grinned. "That could catch on as the in-slang of the week."

"See! I meant totally freak."

"Don't worry, Val. I'm fine."

"Good." Setting her books on the edge of the sink, Val thumbed through a spiral notebook. "I've got the question written out with a couple follow-ups in case we talk to someone who's really hot."

"Which topic did you decide to go with? Kissing on the first date or the on-going crisis in the Middle East?"

"Actually, neither." Val shrugged sheepishly. "Asking a question about world affairs would probably get a blank stare punctuated by a definitive 'duh' from everyone but the geeks. And let's face it, nobody wants to read a column with an interest level that peeks at 'boring much?' "

"You're probably right." Sabrina needed a dynamic extracurricular activity on her school transcript, and a weekly newspaper column was ideal. "Students Speak" had to be great the first time out. "A survey about kissing would get everyone's attention, though."

"True, but a column that even *hints* of 'you-know-what' might make Mr. Kraft 'lotally kreaf.' " Val hesitated, then laughed. "That does have cool slang potential, doesn't it?"

Sabrina nodded. "So what's the topic?"

"Making it socially acceptable for girls to ask boys out on dates at Westbridge High." Val grinned.

Sabrina looked at her askance. "Girls *do* ask boys out, Val. Libby hits on Harvey every chance she gets."

"I know. But cheerleaders can do anything they want and most of us aren't cheerleaders. There's a stigma attached when ordinary girls take the initiative."

Also true, Sabrina thought. If the cheerleaders suddenly decided geeks were cute and brains were cooler than brawn, the new trend would sweep the school before the dismissal bell rang. Everyone would jump on the bandwagon to geekdom without question. An ordinary girl who thought geeks were cool would be branded as desperate and hooted out of the halls.

Warming up, Val began to pace. "The operative concept here is making it socially *acceptable* to—"

The door flew open and Libby blew in, colliding with Val. Val stumbled backward and knocked her books off the sink. Sabrina automatically bent to pick them up. Her gaze focused on the paperback novel lying on top of the scattered pile.

Robinson Crusoe by Daniel Defoe.

Pinggggg!

Shaking off the dizziness, Sabrina took one look at the horde of frenzied natives dancing around a fire and screamed.

Cannibals!

"Shouldn't you pop back to the Other Realm to check on Amanda, Marigold?" Hilda asked. "I sent her back over half an hour ago. She's had enough time to neutralize the child guards on all the electric cauldrons, ransack Witch-Mart, and totally skew the Spell Market Index."

"The Other Realm has survived Amanda for twelve years. One more day won't matter." Scowling at her coffee, Marigold reached for the sugar bowl.

"What happens tomorrow?" Chugging her first cup of coffee, Zelda twitched as the caffeine jolted her system.

"Tomorrow I'm enrolling her in Miss Laura-Lye's boarding school."

"Really?" Hilda grinned.

Click, click, click.

Hilda noticed the faint noise but immediately dismissed it. The news that Marigold was shipping her dangerously precocious daughter off to witch reform school had her full attention.

Zelda pointed her cup full of coffee again. At the same time, the level in the pot on the counter decreased by an equal amount. "That's a little extreme, isn't it?"

"Desperate circumstances call for desperate measures." Sighing despondently, Marigold spooned more sugar into her cup and continued stirring.

"Considering Amanda's offenses, desperate may be an understatement." Hilda shuddered. "All I did was pick a few lousy flowers and I was sent packing off to Old Needle Nose for behavior adjustment."

Even after six centuries, Hilda could still feel the sting of the headmistress's magic wand against her palm. That wasn't the worst of the punishment, though. One never knew what lingering torture Miss Laura-Lye had programmed her wand to dispense on any given day. During her one-year term, she had suffered with all-the-places-you-can't-reach itches, wet-noodle finger droop, seventy-two-hour non-stop hiccup syndrome, ear swelling, and having her tongue tied for real when she had dared to talk back. Miss Laura-Lye's boarding school would do wonders for Amanda—if she survived.

"You didn't just pick a few flowers." Zelda eyed

Hilda narrowly. "You trampled the royal rose garden."

"I was trying to get away from a swarm of crazed hornets."

"After you deliberately rattled their nest, hoping they'd chase the prince."

Click, click, click.

"He was a dweeb." Hilda snorted with disgust. "And a tattletale!"

"Ummm. He never could sit down comfortably after you gave him a tail, either."

Marigold gasped. "You gave a prince a tail, Hilda?"

"Just a little one. A nub, really."

Click. Click. Click.

"It was a well-kept royal family secret." Zelda tapped her chin thoughtfully. "Then, as I recall, you oiled the king's armor."

"It wasn't *my* fault he fell down the castle tower stairs and almost broke his neck," Hilda said indignantly. "If I had *known* he was going to wear it instead of using it to decorate the hall, I wouldn't have oiled the bottom of the boots."

"You're *lucky* you were sent to Miss Laura-Lye's school instead of losing your head." Sitting back, Zelda chuckled. "Why *did* you set the throne on fire, anyway?"

"Because His Royal Highness called me an impertinent peasant who couldn't think her way out of a goatskin bag."

Click, click, click.

"I don't blame you, Hilda." Marigold patted Hilda's hand, then raised her cup. "Your actions were justified even if he was right. Amanda doesn't have stupidity as an excuse."

Zelda's hand clamped over Hilda's arm before she could lift a finger to retaliate for the insult. Catching Zelda's warning look, she nodded a promise not to do anything rash. Her revenge would come in the form of instant inches on Marigold's thighs when she finished her cup of coffee-flavored sugar syrup.

Click, click, click, click, click!

"What *is* that noise?" Hilda cocked her head to pinpoint the sound. "Did you leave the oven on again, Zelda?"

"I haven't used the oven in weeks."

"I've *never* used one." Refilling her cup, Marigold absently began spooning and stirring again. "But then, I've never had to bake a man-dough date because I can't attract a *real* man, either."

Zelda's eyes flashed.

Hilda placed a restraining hand on her shoulder. Zelda couldn't work on the youth formula if she got into a spelling duel with Marigold and lost. "What finally made you decide to take such drastic action with Amanda, Marigold?"

"Arnie." Marigold smiled wistfully. "The new man in my life."

"And I thought the day had already hit rock bottom," Hilda said dryly.

* * *

A hand clamped over Sabrina's mouth, muffling her scream.

"Do be quiet, Miss," a man whispered in a refined British accent. "Or I dare say you'll be the dinner entree rather than those unfortunate blokes in the boat."

Sabrina stopped struggling and nodded that she understood. She had read the classic novel a couple years ago. Even though he was dressed in clothes made of animal skins and had long, unkempt hair and a matted beard, Robinson Crusoe was a civilized man. And after being stranded on the island for twenty-five years, he also knew how to survive.

"There's a good girl." Releasing her, the man turned his attention back to the cannibals.

Sabrina frowned. The main character's calm acceptance of her presence in the story wasn't nearly as weird as how and why she found herself sharing the experience. However, it was obvious that *where* the hallucinations took place was determined by whatever fictional reference was uppermost in her mind when an episode began. At the moment, the critical question was whether she was an active participant or a casual observer.

Glancing down the hill at the clearing in the jungle, Sabrina squirmed. The natives danced and chanted, waving wooden spears and working up an appetite. With any luck, barbecued witch was not on the menu. Since the two unfortunate blokes were now sprawled on a narrow beach waiting to meet their fate as the main course, it seemed likely that the story would unfold as written.

Which meant that one of the prisoners would escape to become Robinson's companion, Friday!

She nudged the worried man kneeling beside her. "That one's going to make a break for it."

"He's hardly in a position to break anything." Robinson scowled at her. "And do stop your chattering. The situation is likely to become unpleasant if we attract their attention, what?"

"Right. Crusoe canapés and Sabrina pâté might be a delicacy they can't resist."

Friday suddenly bolted.

"Blast the luck!" Robinson swore. "He's headed toward my shelter in the grove. I'll not have another moment's peace if those savages discover I'm about on this island."

"Not a problem. Look." Sabrina pointed. "Only three of those guys are following him. You can handle it."

"Yes, but I rather doubt I can handle *them!*"

Looking down, Sabrina saw that the rest of the shouting, spear-carrying dinner party was climbing the steep slope toward where they were hidden. *Hey! That's not in the book,* she thought.

"Run!" Leaping to his feet, Robinson scrambled down a rickety ladder propped against the rocky cliff in front of them.

Sabrina scrambled after him as she ran for her life through the jungle—

Pingggg!

—and stumbled through the door of a school restroom stall, ramming into Libby.

Panting with fear and exertion, Sabrina staggered to the sink and held on until the dizziness passed. When her head cleared, she realized Val and Libby were staring at her. A greater dread than being eaten by cannibals struck.

She hadn't been hallucinating.

She had *popped* in and out of the novel.

Right in front of her best friend and her worst enemy!

☆

Chapter 4

☆

Clumsy much?" Sneering, Libby smoothed out her unwrinkled skirt, then shrieked.

Speechless, Val continued to stare.

Sabrina frantically tried to think of some way to explain her vanishing act.

There wasn't any.

"You *are* sick!" Val almost choked on the words. "I've never seen anyone duck into a john to throw up so fast before."

"Both of you should carry collision insurance!" Red-faced with anger, Libby held up a hand. A delicate black rose adorned the tip of nine of her long, ivory-colored nails. The tenth tip was missing. "You broke my nail! I just had them done. Do you have any idea how much sculpted nails cost at the Saucy Salon?"

Sabrina shifted her gaze between the two girls, hardly daring to believe that neither one of them had actually *seen* her disappear into thin air.

"I bet you've got that flu that's going around, Sabrina." Val paled. "Either we'll gross out all our survey subjects because you're sick to your stomach, or I have to do the interviews myself!"

"I don't have the flu, Val. It must have been something I ate." Sabrina was pretty sure she didn't have Pollyanna Plague, either. If random popping was a symptom, Salem would have warned her so she could avoid any messy complications.

"Who's going to pay for *this?"* One of the unbroken nails fell off as Libby waved her hand. A pained squeal caught in her throat.

"Maybe the Saucy Salon should give you a refund," Val said. "I'll sign an affidavit swearing it just fell off for no reason."

"That's not going to help me today, you freak!" Collecting herself, Libby gently picked up the enameled casualty.

"You can have one of mine!" Prepared to make any sacrifice to appease Libby, Val held out her hand for inspection.

Libby glanced at Val's shorter, polished, but undecorated nails, then laughed as she turned to leave. "Not. Purple is so passé."

"Maybe Mrs. Quick has some glue!" Sabrina flinched as Libby let the door slam behind her.

"Do you ever feel like you've got a sign on your forehead that says 'Disaster, Strike Here'?" Val asked.

"In flashing green neon."

"I think I'll go after Libby and apologize." Grabbing her books, Val headed out.

"Apologize for what?"

"Everything!" The door banged closed.

Sabrina sighed, remembering Salem's warning about sending disaster an open invitation.

Or maybe her smug confidence about not having to worry about a surprise test over the weekend had been too inviting for the Quizmaster to pass up!

And maybe this pop quiz was literally a *pop* quiz!

For what purpose?

The first bell rang.

Gathering her things, Sabrina hesitated. Staying in school seemed like a really bad idea under the circumstances, especially since the uncontrolled popping was related to books. Westbridge High was full of them! Besides, if Aunt Hilda hadn't seen her note on the bathroom mirror, Salem might still be a cookie jar in some as yet undetermined location.

She tried to pop herself home—

No ping.

No pop.

No detour into classic fiction.

She remained in the restroom.

Click, click, click.

Click. Click. Click.

Click, click, click.

Don't any of you people recognize Morse code when you hear it?

Frustrated and tired of blinking SOS with his hard, plastic-doll eyes, Salem glared at the three women seated around the kitchen table.

"Charming doesn't even *begin* to describe Arnie."

Zelda yawned.

Hilda smiled tightly through clenched teeth.

"But another week of Amanda's pranks and he might have a nervous breakdown. I'm not about to let her ruin our relationship or drive Arnie crazy."

"Of course not," Hilda said. "It's not like Arnie is a blood relative and fair game."

Salem fumed. Their total lack of situational awareness was astounding. He had foolishly expected Hilda and Zelda to realize he was missing by now! Or that there was a ceramic cat cookie jar on the counter by the refrigerator that neither of them had acquired with money or magic. Throw Amanda into the equation and how hard could the problem be to figure out? Maybe Hilda couldn't add two and two and come up with four, but Zelda certainly could.

Talk about no-duh moments.

Even more upsetting was that Sabrina had abandoned him. She *knew* what Amanda had done!

"Did I mention that Arnie has a chalet in the Alps, a villa on the French Riviera, *and* a castle in Scotland?"

"Twice." Frowning, Hilda pointed her cup and saucer into the sink so hard, they shattered.

Dozing with her chin propped on her hand, Zelda opened one eye, then promptly closed it again.

Marigold started. "Maybe you should make an appointment to have your finger fine-tuned, Hilda. Dr. Digit recommends regular checkups every six months, especially for older witches—"

"Coffee time's over!" With a quick flick of her hand, Hilda sent all the dishes on the table smashing into the sink.

"What?" Zelda's head snapped up.

Now that Zelda was half awake and Hilda had reached her Marigold tolerance threshold, Salem dared hope they might notice him.

Click, click, click, click, click!

Hilda stood up. "Time to get to work, Zelda."

"I'll never hear the end of it if I don't." Yawning, Zelda flicked a limp finger. Her hair combed and curled itself, and her robe was instantly replaced by pants and a stylish red blouse. "But it's a waste of time."

Click! Click! Click-click-click-click-click—click!

"What's a waste of time?" Marigold asked.

Worried that the plastic eyes could only take so much clicking before they broke or jammed, Salem changed tactics. He stared at Hilda and concentrated.

Your cat is a cookie jar.

"Developing a youth formula," Zelda said wearily.

"Really?" Marigold leaned forward, her eyes widening with intense interest.

"You had to tell her!" Throwing up her hands, Hilda pointed the smashed cups and saucers into oblivion.

Salem is missing. Look for the cat.

"I would do *anything* for a youth potion that worked." Sitting back suddenly, Marigold shrugged. "Not that I need one now, you understand."

Hilda zeroed in on the opening. "I'm impressed, Marigold. Not everyone can accept the ravages of age so graciously."

The cat! Look for the cat!

Marigold parried the remark with a swift counterjab. "I'm amazed at how calm you are, Hilda. Once the flabby sags set in, they're impossible to lose. Short of major surgery, of course."

"Flabby?" Hilda bristled. "Beats having skin that looks like a dry lake bed!"

Zelda whistled. "Enough! The bickering stops now, or else."

"Or else what?" Hilda asked.

"I'll spend today surfing the Net instead of working at the labtop," Zelda said.

Forget the labtop! Your cat is a cookie jar! An empty *cookie jar!* Keenly aware of his hollow pottery insides, Salem was stricken with a sudden craving for oyster chip cookies.

"Oh. Well, since you put it that way, I can be nice." Hilda forced a smile. "For as long as it takes, anyway."

"Marigold?" Zelda fixed her seething cousin with a no-nonsense stare.

"All right!" Huffing, Marigold rolled her eyes. "Although I don't understand why you're both so upset. I was only stating the obvious."

Hilda kept smiling but the veins in her neck popped out with the effort.

The cat! Click, click, click! Heeeeelp!

"Then I might as well get started." Rising, Zelda sighed. "But the *only* reason I'm doing this is to prove once and for all that it *can't* be done."

"But you'll try everything you can think of, right?" Hilda asked as she followed Zelda out the kitchen door.

"Yes, Hilda. I promise."

No! Don't go!

Marigold waited until the two sisters were out of sight before she pointed up a mirror. Her frown deepened as she scrutinized her reflection and plucked a gray hair.

You're gorgeous, Marigold! And famished. You desperately want a cookie!

"I do *not* look my age." The mirror popped out as Marigold tossed it over her shoulder and snapped her fingers. "I look older!"

A cookie will make you feel better!

Rising slowly, the troubled witch began to pace about the kitchen. As she passed the counter by the refrigerator, Salem blinked frantically.

Click! Click, click, click, click!

The sound attracted Marigold's attention and Salem's nonexistent heart fluttered as she gazed into his plastic eyes.

Click, click, click, click!

"How quaint. Must be one of those novelty gizmos mortals find so amusing. I always knew Hilda and Zelda had no taste."

None whatsoever! So why don't you go insult them about the kitty cookie jar they don't know they have! Then maybe they'll take the hint and rescue me!

Sighing, Marigold looked toward the dining room door.

Yes!

"Zelda may have no sense of style, but she does have brains." Marigold hesitated, then hurried toward the door. "If anyone can find the elixir of youth, she can!"

Remember the cookie jar!

Seconds passed and no one came rushing back into the kitchen. One minute. Two minutes.

Closing his plastic eyes, Salem sobbed. Trapped in ceramic limbo and forsaken by everyone who was supposed to care, he had to face the possibility that he might spend the rest of his cat life as a cookie jar, doomed to wander from one garage sale to another for a hundred years.

His only consolation was that Hilda had sent Amanda back to the Other Realm, making the mortal world safe for everyone else again.

Folding her arms, Amanda leaned back against the headboard of Sabrina's bed to survey the results of her handiwork.

"I like it."

"Who-whoo." The owl perched on the bedpost blinked.

"I'm glad you agree, Mr. Owl." Totally satisfied, Amanda frowned. The Midnight Swamp motif suited her mood and provided the perfect atmosphere for plotting her next move.

Floating on murky water, Sabrina's bed bobbed gently as an alligator swam by. A large snake slithered down the trunk of a gnarled cypress tree in the far corner. Spanish moss hung in grotesque gobs from the canopy—formed by the upper branches of several trees—that stretched across the ceiling. A pair of yellow eyes stared out of the gloom in the turret alcove. In another corner, Sabrina's dresser was slowly being sucked into a pool of quicksand.

Crickets chirped.

Cicadas sang.

A black crow cawed.

A frog croaked.

Locating the large amphibian on a lily pad, Amanda pointed up a swarm of flies for his lunch. The frog ignored them.

"Pouting doesn't suit you, Gerald. I thought you'd enjoy a little outing in your natural habitat."

"Rivet ruck!"

"Suit yourself." Stretching out, Amanda watched a spider spin a web between the ceiling and a twisted, leafless twig. "But I'm not changing you back until you promise to sell me any potion ingredients I want! Including the ones that are marked Licensed Witches Only."

"Rivet! Rivet, rivet!"

"So what? *I* don't care if the Witches Council revokes your permit to sell regulated spell supplies if you get caught!"

Thhh-whap! A fly disappeared with a flick of Gerald's tongue. Leaping off the lily pad, he swam to the far bank and burrowed into the mud.

"Be a frog forever! See if I care!"

She didn't, of course. At the moment, all she cared about was *not* going to boarding school. Unfortunately, there wasn't anything she could do about it. The insidious minds that had set up the witch rules had given parents the power to counter their children's spells and enforce their parental authority.

Marigold could turn Gerald back into a shopkeeper with a snap of her fingers, except that she was so totally smitten with Arnie she didn't realize Gerald wasn't really a frog.

Arnie.

Amanda grimaced. He was *so* sweet, handsome, generous, and thoughtful he made her nauseous. He also wasn't Harold.

Not that she had ever liked her father much, either. She had tried everything she could think of to drive Arnie away, including stuffing his socks with scorpions, spiking his drinks with waking nightmare powder, and sprinkling his nose hairs with sneeze-and-grow. Nothing had deterred him from his romantic pursuit of her mom. Not toenail rot, magnetized mouth, or loose goose feather tickling attacks. Her desperate and lovesick mother had begged her to stop and give him a chance.

Not!

She had expected Marigold to punish her by confiscating her Dustbuster so she couldn't fly or installing truancy wards so she couldn't leave the house unescorted.

She certainly hadn't expected a one-way ticket into exile.

And now someone was going to be very sorry.

Her mother, Arnie, and especially Miss Laura-Lye.

The sound of water lapping gently around the open closet doors drew Amanda's vengeful attention. One by one, she ripped the hangers off the bar and dropped Sabrina's wardrobe into the swamp.

Chapter 5

Miniaturized and wedged between an armrest and the front seat of a car, Sabrina saw a mechanical toad with enormous eyes fling itself at a six-legged mini-machine that vaguely resembled a beetle with lethal pincers.

"And I left my insect repellant at home."

Fascinated and terrified, she had no choice but to wait, watch, and hope the strange combatants didn't notice her. She silently rooted for the toad thing.

Aside from being an unwilling, on-the-scene spectator of the ghastly drama, her situation in the real world had taken a definitive turn for the worse. There was a good chance she would be seen popping back into school. Miscalculating the timing of her exit from the restroom to get to history class, she had rushed through the door as the period bell rang. She had almost bumped into Gordie as he strolled down the hall with his nose buried in a book called *Bug Park* by James P. Hogan. Totally engrossed in the story, he had just kept walking.

And she had popped into the battle of the bug-bots.

Grimacing as the creatures locked heads, she groaned when the beetle struck one of the toad's eyes.

The beetle glanced toward her position.

"Uh-oh. There's never a SWAT team around when you need one!"

Raising her books to defend herself, Sabrina winced—

Pingggg!

—and popped back into school.

Alone in the empty hallway, Sabrina lowered her books and frowned. "So who won?"

Curious, she raced for the open classroom door across the hall. She knew how *Pollyanna* and *Robinson Crusoe* ended, but she'd have to get *Bug Park* from the library to find out what happened—as soon as she didn't have to worry about popping in and being torn apart by mechanical micro-beasties. Right now, she was late.

But so was Ms. Chalmers.

"Hey, Sabrina!" Grinning, Harvey leaned forward as Sabrina slid into her seat. "Where have you been? I haven't seen you all morning."

"I've been here." Smiling brightly, Sabrina kept her gaze fastened on Harvey's face, avoiding the pile of books in front of him. He was still reading Dickens's *A Tale of Two Cities* for English and she'd probably pop into line just ahead of Sidney Carton on his way to the guillotine. "And there!"

She had been making herself scarce between classes, hiding in restrooms until just before the final bell rang. Except for her chance encounter with Gordie's science-fiction novel, her precautions were working. Textbooks didn't seem to have the same effect as novels, so she hadn't popped into the chemical formula for hydrochloric acid during science or found herself hanging out in a trig equation waiting to be assigned a value in math. However, she couldn't pop home, either.

"I'm really looking forward to tonight, Sabrina."

"I am, too," Sabrina said, hoping the popping problem would be solved long before eight o'clock. An image of roller-skating into the pages of the latest best-selling thriller flashed into Sabrina's mind. Getting caught in the cross fire between renegade cops and mastermind criminals or confronting some terrifying paranormal phenomenon wasn't how she wanted to spend Friday night. If the problem persisted, maybe she could talk Harvey into watching videos at home.

"I, uh, don't usually admit this, but I really like roller-skating." Harvey shrugged. "There's just something about zooming around and around with the music and the lights and all. It's kind of like going off into another world for a while, you know?"

"Oh, uh—yeah. I've so been there." Sabrina sighed. Videos were out. The roller rink was in.

Harvey sat back as Ms. Chalmers bustled into the room. "Well, we're off to the wars."

"What war? I'm not combat ready!" Sabrina paled. What if the key element was words! Her history book was full of dangerous but true stories about the past.

"I think we're just expected to read about Edward I taking over Scotland. Not join the ranks."

"But I'm eligible for the draft!"

Noticing that her math book was on top of her world history text, Sabrina left it there. Ms. Chalmers loved to lecture, and for once she would be glad to listen to the woman's monotonous, nasal drone. Unless the teacher specifically mentioned the title of a novel, as Salem had done with *Polly*—whoops, don't go there—she'd probably be okay.

"As you all know, or should know, the English king Edward I claimed the throne of Scotland in 1291 when the Scottish king died, leaving no heir." Ms. Chalmers peered at the class as though she expected someone to admit that they didn't know.

Sabrina held her breath and her position in the classroom.

"Who can tell me the name of the man who led the Scottish revolt against him?" Ms. Chalmers asked.

No one volunteered an answer.

Sighing, Ms. Chalmers walked over to the light switch, then raised a remote control and turned on a TV and VCR sitting on a cart in the corner. "Perhaps this will refresh your memories."

As the room darkened and a battle sequence from a movie appeared on the screen, Sabrina crossed her fingers. She didn't pop.

"Oh, I know!" Jill, a cheerleader and one of Libby's faithful companions, called out. "Mel Gibson!"

A wave of laughter rippled through the room.

Harvey whispered, "William Wallace in *Braveheart.*"

"Yes, I know." Relaxing, Sabrina glanced over her shoulder—

Pinggggg!

—and saw thousands of crudely dressed men and boys covering the grassy hill behind her. Carrying leather shields, swords, axes, wooden spears, and farm implements, they stood ready to fight and die for Scotland and the courageous man riding on the plain before them.

Sabrina stared. Mounted on a black horse, his long hair tied back off his forehead and braided on the sides, his face painted warrior blue, with a broad sword strapped to his back and a faded tartan thrown over a leather breastplate, the man was magnificent.

"It *is* Mel Gibson!" Beaming with delight, Sabrina nudged the man on her right and pointed. "That's Mel Gibson."

"Mind yer tongue, lass!" The scruffy-looking man's hand tightened on the hilt of his knife. "I dunno know who this Gibson may be, but that's the Wallace himself and none other!"

"Aye. So he says." The man behind her sighed. "But it's going back to our farms we should be and nay followin' a daft man into a battle that's already lost."

"It's winnin' we'll be this day!" The man on Sabrina's left rattled his shield, spraying her with loosened dirt and miscellaneous animal hairs.

"Good thing I wore boots. Although my make-up's all wrong. Blue face-shadow just never quite caught on where I come from. . . ."

As the men pressed closer to hear Wallace speak, Sabrina wrinkled her nose. Deodorant wouldn't be invented for another six hundred years, and the odor rising from thousands of unwashed bodies packed so close together was staggering. All this crowd had to do was stand upwind and let Edward's army drop from the stench.

". . . fireballs from my eyes and a lightning bolt from my . . ."

Raising an eyebrow, Sabrina glanced at her finger. She was tempted to point up a few fireballs and lightning bolts, but refrained. She didn't know if her magic worked here, but if it did, they burned or stoned witches in the late thirteenth century. Besides, it wasn't in the script.

As she listened to Wallace's impassioned speech, Sabrina turned her thoughts to her own predicament. She had just vanished from her history class, which might not be a huge problem as long as the room was dark and everyone's attention was riveted on the TV screen when she popped back.

Which shouldn't be too many seconds from now, considering how long she had stayed in the other scenarios.

TV screen!

Was she part of the scene everyone was watching?

Events were playing out exactly as they had in the movie, although the men around her weren't acting like extras. They certainly didn't smell like them.

There wasn't a camera or a production crew in sight, either.

Looking up, she saw Wallace and the nobles riding back from the failed negotiations with the English army. The battle was going to start any minute.

"Why couldn't I have popped into one of the romantic scenes in the beginning?" she moaned.

A hundred archers assembled in front of the king's mounted knights.

"How will being trampled or impaled make me a better witch?"

"Who's a witch?" The man on the left snapped his head around to eye her suspiciously.

Shaking her head, Sabrina laughed. "I meant *which* would you prefer? Being trampled or impaled?"

"It's a mite late to be worryin' about that now, isn't it, lass?"

Hoots and howls erupted as Wallace's assembled forces lifted their kilts in a Celtic display of bravado and disdain.

Sabrina looked skyward. "Now would be a good time!"

Silence fell as Wallace joined his men in the front line and the archers raised their bows.

Sabrina fast-forwarded her memory of the movie. The archers would fire twice. Then the English commander would send the knights charging forward with lances leveled. Wallace would stand fast until he signaled his men to raise the long wooden pikes that would take out all the king's horses and all the king's men.

"I *hate* that part!" Wincing, Sabrina ducked down with her comrades as the first barrage of arrows fell from the sky. Cowering under their overlapping shields, she covered her ears to drown out the sound of—

Pinggggg!

—laughter.

"What exactly are you doing under your desk, Sabrina?" Ms. Chalmers asked.

"Uh—" Crawling into the aisle, Sabrina stood up and shrugged. "Sorry. I just *really* get into movies."

Sitting on the edge of her seat by the labtop, Hilda watched Zelda think and ignored the phone.

Marigold stopped pacing to glance toward the kitchen. "Isn't someone going to answer that?"

Staring off into space, Zelda didn't respond.

Hilda blinked, remembering that she had forgotten to rewind the answering machine tape after Willard had filled it with apologetic messages following their last argument. It wasn't picking up and neither was Salem. Apparently, the cat was taking a longer than usual morning nap.

The phone rang and rang.

"Hilda!" Marigold stamped her foot. "Answer the phone before it drives me insane!"

"It's highly improbable the phone will succeed where Amanda failed, Marigold. Assuming she failed." Hilda's unwavering gaze remained on Zelda. "Get a grip. It'll stop."

Collapsing in another chair, Marigold took a deep breath. "I'd answer it, but I don't want anyone to think I've joined a spinster support group."

"Always a spinster, never a divorcee!" Hilda said lightly. Zelda had been contemplating her alchemy research notes and cross-referencing spells on MagicNet all morning. Now that she had finally started mixing a potion, Hilda didn't want to miss anything.

The phone rang two more times.

"Answer the phone, Hilda." Zelda jotted down a note, then stared at the pad. "That constant ringing is ruining my concentration."

"Twenty-two rings is rather persistent, isn't it?

Either Sabrina's in trouble or it's another long-distance carrier trying to get us to switch." Jumping up, Hilda hesitated as Zelda reached for a vial.

Marigold started biting her nails.

"And please, stop fidgeting, Marigold." Adding a pinch of ground vulture talon to the beaker on the Bunsen burner, Zelda frowned. "It's almost as distracting as Hilda's glassy-eyed stare of breathless anticipation."

"I'll get the phone." Dashing into the kitchen, Hilda picked up. "Hello?"

"Is Sabrina all right?" Zelda shouted.

"This is Other Realm Communications!"

Click! Click! Click!

With a quick glance around the kitchen for the annoying noise, Hilda covered her exposed ear. "If this is a switch pitch, we're not interested."

The ORC salesperson pitched a flat ten-cents-a-minute rate for calls between the mortal and the magic realm anyway.

"Sorry. We already have that plan through WT&T." Hilda paused, her eyes widening with sudden interest. "Spell ID? You're kidding."

Click, click, click, click. Click!

Hilda listened for another minute, then refused the new service. Prank spell calls were rare and not worth the additional expense. Besides, if ORC had the new technology, WT&T would have it soon, too, and competition would drive the rates even lower. She'd hold out for the free Spell ID box and installation.

Click! Click! Click!

"Where *is* that noise coming from?"

Click, click, click, click, click!

Hanging up, Hilda pointed at the receiver. "Phone's busy until further notice."

With that distraction eliminated, she turned her attention to the kitchen. Like a dripping faucet, the incessant clicking was getting on her nerves. She didn't notice the unfamiliar cookie jar until she looked behind the refrigerator.

"Where did you come from?"

Click, click, click!

Hilda started, then leaned closer to study the plastic doll eyes. "Weird. I wonder if Zelda finally opened that April Fool's present Wally Barton gave her twelve years ago?"

Click, click!

Zelda had stopped dating the practical joker when his pranks exceeded the boundaries of good taste. Wally had sent the present two months later. Afraid to open it or throw it away in either realm lest some other unsuspecting soul find it, they had stashed it in the attic.

Click, click, click.

Or maybe Zelda had bought it and neglected to tell her. Hilda didn't want to interrupt her sister's youth potion experiments to find out. The cookie jar seemed harmless enough, except for the blinking eyes, which were getting old fast.

"Maybe it runs on batteries."

Click, click.

Hilda checked the bottom, the back, and the inside. There was no battery compartment or any other mechanism to account for the blinking. Unless—

"You're not really a cookie jar, are you?"

Click, click.

"Click, click." Hilda frowned. "Does that mean 'no'?"

Click!

"I'll take that as a yes. Next question. Were you a handsome prince?"

Pause.

Click, click.

"Oh." Disappointed, Hilda shrugged. "So how long have you been a cookie jar?"

Click, click, click, click, click—

"Sorry. I forgot you're communication challenged." Intrigued, Hilda rephrased for a yes or no answer. "Were you a cookie jar yesterday?"

Click, click.

"No, huh? Do I know you?"

Click.

"I do? Are you a witch?" When the cookie jar didn't answer, Hilda frowned thoughtfully. Who did she know who wasn't a witch, but was—or had been? "Salem?"

Click.

"Is Amanda responsible for this?"

Click.

"Sit tight, Salem. I'll zap her right back here to reverse the spell."

Click, click.

"No? Why not? Do you *like* being a fat black jar with a removable head?"

Click, click.

"I can't reverse it! I'm not Amanda's parent—" Hilda slapped her forehead. "Marigold's right in the other room—"

"Eureka!" Zelda whooped in the dining room.

"She did it!" Giggling, Hilda whirled and ran for the door. "Ponce de Leon couldn't find the fountain of youth, but we just hit a gusher on College Street!"

Click, click, click, click, click!

☆

Chapter 6

☆

Busy? How can it be busy?" Irritated, Sabrina stared at the pay phone. "What happened to call waiting?"

"You're waiting, aren't you?" Libby didn't slacken her pace as she breezed by with Mr. Kraft.

Sabrina raised her finger to spin a tangled rat's nest in Libby's hair complete with rat, then thought better of it when Mr. Kraft paused to look back.

"No loitering in the halls, Sabrina."

"I'm not loitering, Mr. Kraft. I'm using the phone."

"You're a teenager. Loitering and using the phone are the same thing."

"The line's busy. Aunt Hilda is so popular

lately." Smiling, Sabrina derived a few seconds of intense satisfaction when Mr. Kraft flinched.

Replacing the receiver, Sabrina sagged against the wall as the vice-principal disappeared around the corner. Aunt Hilda and Mr. Kraft's stormy relationship was not of immediate concern. Since she was cut off from her aunts, Salem might still be a cookie jar sitting on a thrift store shelf and she'd have to figure out the popping puzzle on her own.

So far, she didn't have a clue.

Moving toward the nearest closet to wait out the lunch hour, Sabrina started thinking. Most of the characters she had met had little in common except a determination to fight back in grim situations against overwhelming odds—win or lose. She suspected the same was true of the mechanical toad thing in the book Gordie was reading.

But how did that apply to her?

Everything had been going great until she had started making unexpected side trips into books and TV.

How could she pass a test if she didn't understand the question? And why hadn't the Quizmaster shown up to explain it?

"Good questions!" Sabrina changed course for her locker to get her Witch's Handbook. Since the Quizmaster hadn't given her any guidelines, solving the popping problem had just become an open-book test.

"Come on, Sabrina!" Rolling her eyes, Val ran to

meet her. "We've only got forty-five minutes for lunch!"

"I'm skipping lunch today, Val."

"So am I. It wouldn't be polite or professional to conduct a student survey between bites, would it? Like I can live with everyone thinking I'm eccentric, but I'd never survive gross."

Focused on her own problem, Sabrina had completely forgotten about the "Students Speak" column. "I've got an emergency I really have to take care of, Val."

"An emergency?" Val blinked. "Just like that? Wham! No warning or anything?"

"Emergencies usually are sudden and unexpected."

Frantic, Val grabbed Sabrina's arm. "Is it a matter of life or death?"

"No, not exactly—"

"Then it can wait. Because if we don't get to the cafeteria to do those interviews, I'm going to die of a major anxiety attack before the next bell rings."

"But—" Sabrina grunted as Val shoved a clipboard into her hand and yanked her arm to get her motivated.

"Libby's already there watching the clock and smiling. If we screw this up, I just know she'll use it to convince Mrs. Quick to make her editor. And I'll end up soliciting ads for the classifieds!"

"Right." Sighing, Sabrina gave in. Val's imploring gaze had the same effect on her as water had on the Wicked Witch of the West. She melted.

Besides, the cafeteria didn't have a TV and everyone was too interested in food and their social lives or lack thereof to talk about books. And since her term paper was finished, she could study her Handbook in study hall next period.

All things considered, she had a better than even chance of making it through lunch without disappearing.

"Now there's a prelude to doom," Sabrina muttered as she followed Val through the cafeteria door. "That's probably what Amelia Earhart thought, too."

"Hey, Sabrina!" Harvey waved her over to their usual table.

Val arrived two steps ahead of her. "Sorry, Harvey. Sabrina's got work to do."

"I could start by asking Harvey the survey question," Sabrina suggested. "To get me warmed up."

Harvey frowned. "This isn't about world politics or something else of vital national importance that I don't know anything about, is it?"

"No, it's about a school social issue," Sabrina said. "Do you think it should be socially acceptable for girls to ask boys out at Westbridge High?"

"No!" Rolling his eyes, Harvey leaned back. "Absolutely not."

"What?" Sabrina couldn't believe her ears.

"Why not?" Val asked vehemently. "I mean, it's okay for cheerleaders. Why not for everyone?"

"Because it's hard enough to deal with now, when it's not totally cool. I mean, what does a guy do when he wants to say 'no' because he really can't stand the girl who asks?"

"Say 'no'?" Sabrina checked the hint of sarcasm in her tone. Harvey had learned it was better to decline an unwanted invitation than accept when Libby had asked him to a dance last year. At least, she thought he had learned.

"Easy for you to say. Boys don't cry in front of you when they're rejected."

"That's a totally sexist remark, Harvey." Val flashed him an indignant frown. "I never burst into tears until I'm alone!"

"What's this survey for, anyway?" Harvey frowned as Val continued scribbling on her clipboard.

"The Westbridge Lantern."

"Well, don't quote me, okay?"

Val stared at him. "What good is a newspaper survey if I can't print the answers to the questions?"

Sabrina didn't ask the question that was on the tip of her tongue. She was absolutely positive Harvey had always been honest with her. "Guess I'd better get busy."

"Catch you later!" Harvey grinned at Sabrina, then turned back to Val. "You're not gonna quote me, are you? Going to school with one woman scorned is about all I can handle."

Positioning herself in the far corner, Sabrina cautiously scanned her side of the room and relaxed. None of the girls at the nearest table were reading. Keeping the clipboard, she set her books aside and approached three sophomore girls who were discussing the merits of gradual changes in fashion styles versus costly radical shifts.

"So if I want to look hot and totally now, I'm so busy baby-sitting so I can afford the latest styles, I don't have time to go anyplace where looking hot and so today matters!" Becky Sullivan, a girl with ultrashort red hair and freckles, sighed. "Except school."

"Hey! Have you got a minute?" Sabrina asked.

"Why?" The redhead frowned suspiciously.

"I'm doing a student survey for the school newspaper and I'd like to get your opinion on a topic of vital social significance."

"Uh-huh." Becky's frown deepened. "What's the topic?"

"Should the student body agree to make it socially acceptable at Westbridge High for girls to ask boys out?"

"You're asking me?" Cheeks flushed and blue eyes blazing, Becky started to rise. "Are you implying that a boy wouldn't ask *me* for a date? That is such an insult!"

"No! I'm insulting everyone. I mean, asking everyone."

Jennifer Briggs, who was sitting across from Becky, pushed her glasses back into position on her nose, then glared at Sabrina. "I don't have time to date. I have a 4.0 grade average to maintain because I'd rather go to MIT than waste my time with boys who'd probably turn me down if I asked them out, anyway. So what's the point?"

"Well, I have it on good authority that boys are afraid to say no." Sabrina paused, baffled by their hostile stares. "But you have a valid opinion, so why not take the opportunity to express it in print?"

"My opinion is that I don't care one way or the other." Shaking her head, Jennifer pulled a paperback out of her book bag.

Sabrina inhaled sharply, then exhaled slowly. A book titled *Particle Physics: Theories and Applications* wasn't apt to promote popping.

"Actually, I think making it okay to ask boys out is a good idea." The petite brunette beside Jennifer shrugged.

Jotting that down on her response sheet, Sabrina nodded. "And your name is—?"

"I don't want to be quoted!" Appalled, the brunette shrank in her seat. "Then everyone would think nobody ever asks me out!"

"No one will know it's your answer," Sabrina said. "We're only using initials."

Becky grinned. "Her name is Yvonne Ursula Conklin-Klein. In initials that spells Y.U.C.K. and all her friends know it."

"I see." Sabrina paused. If everyone reacted to Val's question like Harvey and these girls, they wouldn't have enough material to write a filler paragraph. "So tell me—how do you feel about the situation in the Middle East?"

All three girls stared at her blankly.

"Middle East High?" Becky asked. "What's the name of their football team?"

"Never mind." Smiling tightly, Sabrina moved on to a table of junior boys. "Hi, guys! Can I ask you something?"

Swallowing, Ted Adams squeezed a "sure" in before he took another bite of his tuna fish sandwich. As Sabrina had found out when she had been a boy for a while, being gross was not repulsive to males. They wore it like a badge of honor.

"How do you feel about making it socially acceptable for girls to ask boys out at Westbridge High?"

Gagging, Ted almost coughed up what he had just eaten. Tall and thin, with an overbite, he sputtered with surprise. "Why? Are you going to ask me out?"

"No. I'm conducting—"

"I thought you and Harvey were an exclusive, Sabrina," Jake Fontrane said.

"We are. Sort of." Even though they had stopped going steady because she had to concentrate on school and getting her witch's license, Sabrina wasn't interested in anyone but Harvey. Most of the time, anyway. This was *not* an exception.

"Forget Harvey!" Wadding up his napkin, Ted threw it at Jake, then smiled at Sabrina. "I'd love to go out with you, Sabrina. When?"

"No, I'm doing a survey—"

"Then why did you ask?" Disappointed and

embarrassed, Ted quickly fell back, regrouped, and launched a counteroffensive. "Do you get some kind of cheap thrill from ripping a guy's heart out and shoving it back in his face?"

"No!" Calming herself, Sabrina tried to explain. "That was the survey question for a new feature in the school paper."

"Oh, well! Being stomped on and crushed for public consumption makes me feel so much better!"

"Okay, okay." Backing off, Sabrina caught a glimpse of Libby smirking. Cancel retreat. "Can we start over?"

"No, thanks. I've reached my emotional trauma saturation point for the day." Ted resumed stuffing food into his mouth.

Exasperated, Sabrina tossed her pen in the air.

"Yeah. Better lay off, Sabrina." Jake grinned. "Or Ted will be looking for a shrink."

"Or calling Frasier for advice." Lonnie Ellis held his hand to his ear like a phone. "This is Dr. Crane and—"

Squatting down, Sabrina reached for the pen as it rolled under the table.

Pingggg!

"—you're on the air."

Springing upright when the dizziness passed, Sabrina stared at Dr. Frasier Crane. Seated at his desk at the radio station, he spoke into a microphone.

"Hello? Are you there? Sorry. No heavy breathing allowed." Slowly raising his eyes, Frasier started when he noticed Sabrina. "How did you get in here?"

"My fault," Roz said from the control room. "I didn't see her sneak by. But since we don't have anyone else standing by, go for it. Or deal with the dead air. Your choice."

"Well!" Frasier's disconcerted smile segued into a worried frown as he warily eyed Sabrina. "You're not here because you're holding a grudge about some ridiculous advice I gave you that backfired, are you?"

"Uh, no. I just . . . popped in!"

"Good." Wiping his brow, Frasier settled into character. "And you popped in because—?"

Sabrina hesitated, then decided it couldn't hurt to talk. Frasier wouldn't blab about her peculiar troubles all over school. "That's just it. I have this popping problem."

"Popping corn? Popping soda-can tabs? Popping the question? No, wait. Don't tell me." Puzzled, Frasier paused to nibble his knuckle. "Poppin' fresh dough!"

"No, popping into novels, movies, situation comedies. Whatever happens to be the topic of conversation at the time. *Ping* and I'm there! Unless I've been there before."

"So you have a perpetual popping habit."

Sabrina nodded. "It's faster, cheaper, and infinitely safer than public transportation."

Intrigued, Frasier sat back and rubbed his chin.

"And my show was the topic of conversation that made you pop in here?"

"Yes. During lunch at school."

"Cool! We're *pop*-ular with teenagers!" Frasier gave Roz a thumbs up, then spoke to Sabrina in a conspiratorial hush. "Bad puns and low ratings give me nightmares."

"*Pun*-ctuated nightmares are the worst," Sabrina said.

Frasier either didn't hear, chose to ignore, or didn't get her bad joke as he continued with his own train of thought. "When I have falling dreams, I see descending numbers carved into the side of the cliff as I plummet to the ground. It's a long fall from the top."

"Yeah." Sabrina sighed. "I can relate."

Nodding, Frasier leaned forward. "So tell me, how long has this popping problem been a problem?"

"Since this morning. Everything was fine until I tried to pop myself to school and ended up playing a scene with Pollyanna in a book. Then I popped into a couple other books and a movie."

"Uh-huh. And what do you think might be causing this somewhat strange phenomenon?"

"Well, at first I thought I had Pollyanna Plague. But then I realized that if uncontrolled popping was a symptom, my cat would have told me, right?"

"Oh, of course." Frasier cast a sidelong glance at Roz.

From the corner of her eye, Sabrina saw Roz

make a she's-totally-bonkers circling motion near her head. However, talking about the problem *was* a relief, and she didn't care if she sounded certifiable.

"It could be a pop quiz, though. The Quizmaster has this really annoying habit of catching me off guard. He always catches me when I do something wrong, too, which is even more annoying."

"I see." Putting on his serious, I'm-the-doctor face, Frasier sighed. "In my professional opinion, you're either suffering from delusions that manifest themselves in fictional scenarios because you've been deeply hurt or disappointed in real life, or you're totally bored with the mundane routine of being an ordinary, trauma-ridden teenager."

"I don't think so. In real life I'm a witch. Anything is possible, and there's no such thing as boring routine."

"A witch. Did I mention crazy?"

Roz pounded on the window and Frasier quickly recovered his compassionate mike-side manner. "Well then. There's nothing to worry about. You don't need a radio psychiatrist. You need—"

"No! Don't say it!" Sabrina waved to shut him up, but Frasier didn't take the hint.

"—a TV talk—"

Pingggg!

"—show!"

Sitting on a stage, still clutching her survey clipboard, Sabrina cringed as a studio audience applauded the perky blond woman standing in the aisle with a microphone. She had popped into a live local talk show hosted by Margo Crandell.

"Our guests today are people who claim to have paranormal powers," Margo said. "We'll be right back after these messages to see if they can *prove* it."

Oh, boy.

☆

Chapter 7

☆

Many of us believe, although not so many may be willing to admit"—the poised TV host paused for a ripple of laughter—"that strange things happen, things that seem to defy the laws of nature as we understand them."

"Man, is *she* ever covering her bases." Scoffing, the middle-aged woman sitting in the chair beside Sabrina fluffed a mane of wild, waist-length black hair. A long, lacy black dress hung on her thin, bony frame, adding to the skeletal look achieved by white face makeup and overdone black shadows around her dark eyes. Massive dangling earrings and multiple arm bracelets jangled as she leaned closer. " 'Seem to defy'? Give me a break."

"No problem." Coughing and waving away the

overpowering fumes of perfume emanating from the woman, Sabrina didn't pursue the discussion.

"Your thing must be automatic writing, huh?" The woman tapped Sabrina's clipboard with a long, bloodred fingernail.

"Actually, no." Sabrina shook her head emphatically to dispel the assumption that she was a courier for the spirit world. "I'm taking a survey for my school—"

"Cool! You must get the inside story on a bunch of weird stuff from the Otherworld. How's Elvis doing?"

Sabrina sighed, wondering why so many people heard what they wanted to rather than what was said.

"It's the Other *Realm,* and I wouldn't know." Holding her finger up for silence as Margo began introducing her bizarre assortment of guests, Sabrina checked the clock by a monitor. She had been gone much longer this time. With luck she'd pop back soon and arrive under the cafeteria table, hidden from sight.

Of course, she was going to pop *out* on local television, amazing the audience and astounding the amiable star of Westbridge daytime talkdom.

And maybe subjecting herself to more intense scrutiny at school if anyone she knew was watching.

"How many ghosts have you actually helped work through their problems, Jacques?" Standing in the aisle between the stage and the audience,

Margo asked the preposterous question with studied seriousness.

"Six." Sweating under the lights, the pudgy, balding ghost psychic quickly added, "But none that I can document."

"I see." Margo smiled. "Well, Jacques, we may be able to remedy that during the next hour!"

How many of her classmates were homesick and watching the local broadcast today?

Announcing that Jacques was being sent to a Boston landmark with a camera crew to get in touch with the resident ghost, Margo applauded as he left the stage. Then she moved on to Marla, an alleged telekinetic who swore she could pick pockets with the power of her thoughts. To the whooping approval of the studio audience, Margo promised to let her try later on.

Sabrina felt a twinge of mischievous pleasure when she realized that she was probably the only guest who wouldn't disappoint the skeptical spectators. Which solved the problem of what to say when it was her turn.

I can vanish into thin air.

And within the next several minutes she would.

"And next we have Sahara."

The scrawny woman beside Sabrina straightened in her chair, smiled, and waved.

Margo turned to address the audience. "A month ago we had Sahara come to the studio to read my palm and tell my fortune. She wrote down her predictions for my immediate future and sealed them in an envelope. The envelope has been locked in the vault of an unbiased accounting firm, unread, ever since."

Sabrina began to tremble as her fifteen seconds of fame approached. What if Mr. Kraft was a closet Margo fan and had a TV stashed in his office? One of her neighbors was certainly riveted to a TV screen. Her aunts might even be tuned in!

Not likely, but—Sabrina smiled, struck with sudden inspiration. If her aunts were watching for some unfathomable reason, she might be able to get a message through!

"We'll match those predictions with what actually happened to me the past month in a little while."

Sabrina tensed as Margo looked at her, then frowned at someone on the production staff off-camera. A man shrugged and shook his head. She wasn't a scheduled guest, and no one had a clue about her identity. However, Margo winged it with professional calm.

"And last, but not least, we have—" Pleading with her eyes and smiling encouragement, Margo paused so Sabrina could introduce herself.

New plan!

Jumping to her feet, Sabrina looked into the camera and shouted.

"Aunt Hilda! Aunt Zelda! Amanda turned Salem into a cookie jar and I'm—"

Pingggg!

* * *

"What's taking so long?" Hopes dashed because Zelda's earlier "eureka" had not heralded the discovery of a youth elixir, Hilda had maintained her anxious vigil at the labtop.

Zelda peered over the rim of her protective goggles. "People have been trying to unravel the secret of perpetual youth for thousands of years. Pardon me if this takes a few hours."

"Sorry." Folding her hands, Hilda watched Zelda measure precise amounts of old goat hair and shredded sequoia bark into a test tube. "Will you be finished by eight? Before Willard gets here?"

"Yes." Zelda didn't look up from her work as she spoke. "One way or the other."

"What do you mean?"

"If this works, the potion will be done this afternoon. If it doesn't, I'm throwing in the towel." Zelda added two drops of cactus flower nectar, then gently shook the test tube. "The problem is that I'll need a test subject to find out if it works."

Hilda started. "Why is that a problem?"

"Potential side effects."

"Such as?"

Zelda slumped in exasperation. "If I knew that, it wouldn't be a problem."

"Oh." Hilda frowned. "Where's Marigold?"

"Watching her soaps."

"I'll be back."

Stretched out on the couch with her eyes closed, Marigold was paying no attention to the daytime talk show on the TV.

"Has been locked in the vault of an unbiased accounting firm, unread, ever since." Margo's voice blared from the speakers.

"Come on, Marigold. We've got to talk!"

"Huh? What?" Sitting up, Marigold frantically threw her arms over her head. "Is the roof caving in?"

"Not that I noticed." Grabbing the remote off the coffee table, Hilda fumbled for the power button.

Nodding, Marigold massaged her temples. "Amanda hates it when I take afternoon naps. Once I woke up because I was being bombed by paint balloons seeping from the ceiling."

"And last," Margo said, "but not least, we have—"

Hilda hit the power button and the TV screen went blank.

"The worst was being awakened by a screeching Viking who had battered down the front door and was dragging me off by my hair." Marigold sighed. "Although I still have nightmares about the time she gave me chicken pecks."

"Don't you mean chicken pox?"

"No." Marigold shuddered. "Amanda breaded me in corn meal batter, then invited a couple dozen chickens in for a midday snack."

"Well, relax, Marigold. After tomorrow you can nap without fear because Amanda will be with Old Needle Nose. Today you can find eternal youth and beauty"—Hilda hesitated, feigning unease. Tricking Marigold into being the guinea pig for Zelda's youth potion required a devious approach—"if there's any of Zelda's potion left after I test it."

"How come you get to try it first?"

"I *am* her sister. Besides, if I hadn't begged Zelda to look for old alchemy records, she wouldn't be working on a formula at all."

"We'll just see about that!" Brushing past Hilda, Marigold stormed out to argue the point with Zelda.

Pleased that she hadn't lost her skill, Hilda barged into the dining room prepared to follow through with the deception. However, she had failed to take Zelda's scientific ethics into account.

"That's just it, Marigold! I don't *know* what side effects." Losing patience, Zelda clenched her fists and her jaw. "Maybe none. Or maybe it'll turn your skin into an excellent medium for growing mold and mildew!"

Turning slowly, Marigold smiled at Hilda. "You can go first."

Down but not defeated, Hilda wondered aloud. "There's got to be someone else we can trick or blackmail into testing it."

"If you two don't leave me alone, there won't be a potion to test!" Taking a deep breath, Zelda counted to ten under her breath.

"Yes, there will, Zelda," Hilda said. "Once you start on something, you *always* finish."

"What about your cat?" Marigold suggested. "As I recall, he's easily bribed."

Hilda gasped. "Salem!"

"My formula should produce the same results in a cat." Zelda nodded thoughtfully, then wagged a warning finger. "But no tricks. You have to tell Salem about the possibility of side effects and he has to *agree* to be the test subject."

"I forgot all about Salem!" Hilda dashed for the kitchen door. She couldn't believe she had been so focused on recapturing the flawless beauty of youth that she had totally forgotten the helpless cat.

"There's no hurry, Hilda," Zelda said. "I won't be finished for another hour or two."

Hilda looked back. "Yes, but I don't think Salem really wants to spend another two hours being a cookie jar."

"A cookie jar?" Zelda blinked. "Who turned him into a cookie jar?"

Hilda pointed the finger at Marigold.

"I didn't—" Marigold's hand flew to her throat. "Amanda."

"The one and only. Fortunately for us, you're her mother so you can undo the spell. Let's go."

Well, it's about time! Salem mentally huffed as Hilda charged into the kitchen with cousin Marigold.

"I am *so* sorry, Salem." Hilda winced as he commenced to tell her what he thought in frenzied plastic blinking.

Not!

Click, click, click, click, click, click!

If you cared, you wouldn't have forgotten that the faithful family cat was being held hostage in discount-store black glazed pottery!

"I know you've got a right to be upset, *but*—"

Of course I'm upset! I've been a cookie jar all day with no cookies! And what? No milk, either!

Click? Click, click!

"If you don't stop clicking right this instant I'm going to stuff your jar-belly with dog biscuits and set you on the sidewalk by the fire hydrant."

Salem stopped clicking.

"Thank you." Blowing a wisp of hair off her forehead, Hilda motioned to Marigold. "Okay, Marigold. Turn him back."

Marigold started to point, then fisted her finger.

Salem started. *I've got a really bad feeling about this.*

"What's the matter?" Hilda frowned. "You *can* turn him back, can't you?"

"Yes," Marigold said, "but ask him if he'll test the potion first."

The youth potion? Salem's plastic eyelids fluttered nervously. Why should he test it? His feline good looks weren't in danger of deteriorating over the next century.

"Actually, I'm not sure we should use Salem as a laboratory test subject. He's an animal."

Way to go, Hilda!

"Yes, he is, but he's also perfectly capable of making his own decisions, and I'm not going to turn him back until he agrees to try the formula." Folding her arms, Marigold set her mouth in stubborn resolve. "Side effects or no side effects."

What side effects? Dull claws? Matted fur? An aversion to tuna?

"That's blackmail, Marigold."

Click!

"I know. So what? It's not my fault Salem tried to take over the world and Drell turned him into a stupid cat with no magical powers so he can defend himself. Would he give a mouse a break?"

Click, click, click, click, click!

Yes, I would! No mouse has ever *passed these lips! I just like to challenge their will to live every once in a while.*

"Hush, Salem. I'll handle this." Fuming, Hilda raised her finger. "Turn him back now, Marigold, or else."

Yeah! Or else what?

"Or else what?" Marigold thrust her chin forward, daring Hilda to back up the threat.

"Or else I'll erase Amanda's enrollment acceptance to Miss Laura-Lye's boarding school."

I hope that's a bluff! No one deserved an education at Miss Laura-Lye's school more than the ruthless Amanda. On the other hand, Salem reflected, being a cookie jar had little to recommend it as a permanent lifestyle.

"Hilda! You wouldn't dare!"

"How long have you known me, Marigold?"

Marigold took a moment to think about Hilda's ultimatum, then shrugged. "Go for it, Hilda. I can endure Amanda until the next semester starts, but I won't endure growing old another second if I don't have to."

Hilda raised her finger, then frowned uncertainly. "Do I really want to save Amanda from Miss Laura-Lye?"

No! Salem blinked twice. The dismal prospect of remaining in ceramic captivity while Amanda suffered through the head witch's methods in manners seemed like a small price to pay. The malicious little witch would be sixteen before long, and the harmonious order of the universe was at stake.

Torn, Hilda hesitated, her cocked finger trembling with indecision.

"Let the cat decide, Hilda." Marigold looked Salem in the eye. "What'll it be? Cookie jar or laboratory rat?"

Rat? Are you trying to make this decision harder, Marigold?

"Before you answer, Salem," Hilda said, "you should know that Zelda doesn't have a clue what side effects to expect."

"But there may not be any," Marigold added emphatically.

"Right!" Hilda nodded. "Zelda isn't even sure she can make a formula that works. If she fails, you'd be off the hook entirely."

Marigold held up her finger. "Cookie jar?"

No way!

Click, click.

"He said 'no.' " Hilda's grim countenance brightened. "Does that mean you'll be the test subject?"

Click.

"Cat's honor?"

Not taking any chances are you, Hilda? Salem sighed.

Click.

"Was that a 'yes'?" When Hilda nodded, Marigold pointed.

"Cat to jar, a spell was spun.
Now the daughter's deed's undone."

Salem shivered as ceramic and plastic slowly morphed into feline flesh and bone.

"Free at last!" Stretching to work the kinks out of his stiff limbs, Salem purred. "Oh my aching muscles, that feels good. What's for lunch?"

"Is your stomach all you ever think about, Salem?" Hilda asked.

"When you have a hollow stomach, it's hard to ignore. Besides, for all you know, this may be my last meal. I'll have tuna, caviar, a saucer of milk, and oyster chip cookies for dessert."

Flopping down by his bowl as Hilda reached into the cabinet, Salem resigned himself to whatever fate and Zelda's labtop had in store.

At least Amanda wasn't lurking about to complicate things.

Lulled by the slight rocking of the bed on stagnant water, Amanda studied her magical masterpiece. The terraforming of Sabrina's room was a total success.

Her cousin's entire wardrobe hung from the cypress trees, dripping muck and stinking of swamp. Most of her knickknacks were buried in the mud bank with Gerald. The quicksand had totally consumed the desk, and an assortment of reptiles, amphibians, and insects had taken up residence in the chest of drawers. The alligator was lounging on the water-logged settee near the foot of the bed.

Not bad, Amanda thought, confident that her creation couldn't be removed with a mere flick of her mother's finger. She had cleverly used several spells. Although Marigold would try to reverse them all, she was bound to miss something. Exhausted, Amanda fell asleep knowing Sabrina would be stuck with bits and pieces of the Midnight Swamp motif for a while.

Swamp stench was so hard to get rid of, even with magic.

☆

Chapter 8

☆

Popping"—shouting as she vanished from the talk show, Sabrina quickly lowered her voice—"back under the cafeteria table."

Grabbing the pen that had rolled between Ted's feet, Sabrina backed out past a pair of polished high-heeled boots. On her hands and knees, she looked up to see Libby looking down with an amused smirk.

"Now that you've finished cleaning the crumbs off the floor, Sabrina, I'd love to hear how the survey is going."

"It's going great!" Yanking Sabrina to her feet, Val drew her aside. "I know I'm in the high-risk pool for social advancement at Westbridge because we're friends, but I don't think groveling at Libby's feet is going to help."

"Quite the contrary," Libby said. "It's about time Sabrina showed me the respect I deserve."

"Oh." Val smiled. "Well, if it'll make a difference—"

"You are so right, Libby." Dusting herself off, Sabrina discreetly pointed at Libby's boots. "Respect this."

The heels collapsed, throwing Libby off balance. She fell into Ted's lap.

"Man! The girls are just falling all over you today, Ted." Shaking his head, Jake sat back.

"I've got a cheerleader on my lap." Recovering from his initial shock, Ted threw his arms around Libby and shouted. "Hey, everyone! Libby's sitting in my lap!"

"I am not!" Mortified, Libby wiggled to free herself. "Let me go!"

"No problem." Ted shoved his chair back, dumping Libby on the floor as he released his grip and stood up. "But next time you throw yourself at someone, make sure he's interested first!"

Ted's friends at the table whistled and applauded.

Score one for the dating deprived, Sabrina thought with a wry grin as Ted executed a sweeping bow, grabbed his books, and left with his head held high.

Libby silenced the cheers with a scathing look,

then wobbled out the side door, dragging her boot heels and her dignity behind her.

"I'm asleep and dreaming that Libby just got put down in public by a geek, right?" Val asked.

"Put down and totally squashed. Makes you feel all warm and fuzzy inside, doesn't it?"

"No. Not if the Westbridge High social structure is on the verge of collapse." Heaving a heavy sigh, Val followed Sabrina to the corner. "If that happens, what's left to aspire to?"

"A weekly column in the school newspaper?"

"Not if *this* survey is any indication." Val gave her clipboard a disgruntled glance. "The kids I've talked to either don't want to be quoted, have no opinion, or didn't understand the question. Maybe we need an easier question."

"Right," Sabrina scoffed. "The subject of dating practices being beyond the concern of normal teenagers."

"I'm flying blind most of the time."

"We just need a different angle, Val. Let's get together after school to figure something out, okay? Right now, I've got an emergency on hold and I gotta go."

Bolting, Sabrina grabbed her Handbook from her locker and ducked into an empty classroom. Flipping to the chapter on molecular transference, she scanned the topics for popping aberrations—

Pingggg!

—and popped into a sea of upper- and lowercase

letters, punctuation marks, numerals, and other symbols in various fonts and colors.

"Hey! The Handbook isn't fiction! What's the big idea?"

"That's what *I'd* like to know!" Wearing a Hawaiian shirt, baggy shorts, sandals, and glitter-rimmed sunglasses, the Quizmaster popped out of a capital *Q* carrying a glowing orange drink festooned with a purple umbrella.

"Just the man I wanted to see!" Latching onto a large *J* to slow her drift, Sabrina waved.

"Figures! One minute I'm relaxing in the Hesperus Lounge on Ishtar Terra, Venus, watching a glorious volcano eruption and then *poof!* Suddenly I'm consorting with the alphabet in your Handbook!" Draping his arms over the crossbar of a lowercase *T,* the Quizmaster whipped off his sunglasses. "Why?"

"I was just looking something up because I don't have a clue what this pop quiz of yours is all about and *wham!* Here I am. And this isn't even a novel!"

"What pop quiz?" The pitch of the Quizmaster's voice rose in agitation. "I'm not giving you a test!"

"You're *not?*"

"No. I'm on vacation! At least, I was."

"Then how come I'm popping in and out of books and TV for no reason?" Sabrina asked.

"Oh, there's a reason. But I'm not it." Sighing, the Quizmaster took a sip of his drink. "Random popping into fiction, huh? Since when?"

"Right before I left the house this morning. This

is the first time I haven't popped into a story, though." Sabrina's *J* started swinging as she batted away a *B* on a collision course. "What's with all these loose letters?"

"The Handbook *is* a textbook. They're text." The Quizmaster shrugged. "And magic books don't operate under the same rules as those written in the mortal realm."

"I'll say!" Sabrina ducked to avoid a diving *D* as it swooped past chasing a zigzagging *Z*. "This text is totally undisciplined. Why aren't there any words?"

A short distance away a bunch of letters suddenly formed a huddle to confer, then separated into a straight line.

BECAUSE!

"Why should text characters work when nobody's reading them?" The Quizmaster patted twin *M*'s hovering in front of him. "They're always back in position when you need them."

Watching the letters in *BECAUSE* disperse in seven different directions, Sabrina smiled. "Maybe that explains why typos show up in pages that have been proofread a dozen times."

"Nobody's perfect." Kicking his feet, the Quizmaster maneuvered his *K* closer to Sabrina's swaying *J*. "So what happened right before you left the house?"

"Well, Amanda paid us a surprise visit, but—"

"Marigold's Amanda?" The Quizmaster scowled when Sabrina nodded. "I can't *wait* until that little witch is old enough to be accountable for her actions."

"You and everyone else in the Other Realm. And now she's running amok in the mortal world, too."

Arching an eyebrow, the Quizmaster laughed. "And you can't figure out why you're popping control has gone berserk?"

"But she didn't see me!" Grabbing a stationary *G,* Sabrina released the rocking *J.* "She was too busy zapping Aunt Hilda with a prune-face spell."

"And Hilda did what?"

"I don't know. I popped out to school and was detoured to Pollyanna land."

Taking another sip of his nuclear orange drink, the Quizmaster frowned. "Either you're missing something, Sabrina, or Amanda zapped—"

Pinggg!

Popping back into the classroom, Sabrina caught a glimpse of Mr. Kraft walking by the open door with Mrs. Quick. The vice-principal quickly stepped back to gawk.

"You weren't standing there a second ago." Mr. Kraft made the statement with absolute confidence.

"Yes, I was," Sabrina said with equal certainty.

"No, you weren't. I looked into this room as I passed by and *you* were not in it. So how'd you get here?"

"Molecular transference?"

"Oh. Just *beamed* in, did you? From where?" Mr. Kraft asked in a taunting tone. "The Delta Quadrant?"

"More like popped up. From the floor." Picking up her backpack from where she'd dropped it by the desk, Sabrina started for the door before Mr. Kraft said something she'd regret. If she popped out in front of him, he wouldn't be distracted by an honest joke again. "I don't want to be late for study hall."

"You already are." Mr. Kraft pointed to the clock on the wall. "The bell rang two minutes ago."

Sabrina wilted inside. Doing detention today would delay getting home another hour. The longer she stayed in school, the greater the chances that someone would actually see her pop in or out.

"Come *on,* Mr. Kraft!" Mrs. Quick called. "You're late for the school board budget meeting!"

"I'm coming! I'm coming." Mr. Kraft sighed with reluctant resignation. "Sometimes being stranded in the Delta Quadrant seems like an infinitely better alternative than being a high school vice-principal bound for a quarterly budget meeting."

Sabrina fled into the hall as Mr. Kraft trudged toward Mrs. Quick.

"I didn't know you were a *Star Trek* fan, Mr. Kraft." Mrs. Quick's high voice resounded down the empty corridor. "I never miss *Voyager* or *Deep—"*

Pinggg!

Suddenly the center of attention on the bridge of the Starship *Voyager,* Sabrina smiled and waved as all eyes instantly turned toward her. Although she wasn't thrilled to be boldly going where no teenage witch had gone before, at least she hadn't popped into the Dominion War on *Deep Space Nine.*

"We have an intruder," the Vulcan chief of security announced calmly.

"I can see that, Mr. Tuvok. What I want to know is"—rising from the center chair, Captain Kathryn Janeway shriveled Sabrina with her commanding, no-nonsense gaze—"who are you and where did you come from?"

"Sabrina Spellman. Earth."

"Really?" Without shifting her gaze from Sabrina's face, Janeway addressed the handsome ensign at a console on the upper level. "Sensor report, Mr. Kim."

"No ships, space-time continuum distortions, or other anomalies in the immediate area, Captain. Long-range sensors aren't picking up anything, either."

Janeway folded her arms, cocked her head, and regarded Sabrina with guarded curiosity. "Are you a Q?"

"No, but my Quizmaster just popped through a *Q* in my Handbook." Clutching her books to her chest, Sabrina smiled, then coughed self-consciously when no one smiled back.

"Popped through?" Tom Paris looked up from the helm.

Commander Chakotay stepped up behind the captain. "Is this 'popping' similar to how the Q instantaneously transport themselves anywhere in the universe?"

"Yeah!"

"Would you care to demonstrate?" Janeway asked skeptically.

"I would, but the, uh . . . phase whatchamacallit calibrations in my popping gizmo thingie are totally whacked!" Sabrina wiggled her finger.

"Captain." Seven of Nine moved up behind Sabrina and slowly circled her. "The Borg encountered this particular variation of the human species during one of their revelry rituals in the Crab Nebula. We did *not,* however, assimilate them."

Janeway and Chakotay looked at each other in surprise.

"Why not?" Janeway asked.

"They have no technology," Seven answered abruptly.

Chapter 9

Sabrina popped off the *Voyager* bridge in the middle of a fascinating discussion about an incident on the *Enterprise* D. Scurrying to study hall, she wondered what had happened to that Amanda, a teenage girl who had been raised as a human and didn't know she was a Q. Had Amanda embraced her unique existence as Sabrina had when she turned sixteen and found out she was a witch?

Life since then had not been boring, and most of the time it was fun.

Then there are days like today.

Convincing the study hall teacher she had been delayed by Mr. Kraft, Sabrina took her seat and concentrated on solving the popping problem. She stared out the window to avoid the annoying number of novels being read in the room.

Since the Quizmaster wasn't responsible, it seemed more than likely that Amanda had cast the random popping spell. Getting the spell removed wouldn't be hard once her aunts knew about it, either. All they had to do was contact Cousin Marigold to pop in and reverse it. The matter could be settled after school so she could keep her date with Harvey at the roller rink. With only two periods to go, she might be able to stay put for the duration of the school day.

If she didn't talk to anyone, see a novel title or a TV screen or overhear anyone discussing TV, movies, or books.

Which might be a little difficult in seventh-period English, since literature was always the topic.

Faced with the prospect of gallivanting around France with the Three Musketeers or tramping through the colonial American forests with the Deerslayer, Sabrina sighed. Things could be worse, though. At least Amanda had not condemned her to spending a day popping in and out of low-budget horror movies.

Amanda woke up to the shrill sound of shrieks from downstairs. Curious about what awful calamity had befallen her mother and aunts, she tiptoed to the head of the stairs.

"You're sure, Zelda?" Marigold asked.

"As sure as I can be without testing it."

Frustrated because she couldn't see, Amanda popped herself into an old family photograph hanging on the dining room wall to eavesdrop and watch.

Sitting at the labtop, Aunt Zelda held up a beaker of smoking, bubbling, icky yellow stuff. Tense and excited, her mother and Aunt Hilda stood on either side of her, staring at the concoction.

"So that's the elixir of youth," Hilda said in awe.

Zelda nodded. "*If* it works without any adverse side effects."

"Wasn't I supposed to go to the vet for shots today?"

Spotting Salem lying on the sideboard, Amanda frowned. She liked him better as a cookie jar.

"Nice try, Salem," Hilda said, "but you promised to be the test subject and it's time to keep your word."

"I lied." Springing off the sideboard to make a run for it, Salem yowled as Hilda pointed him to a midair halt and zipped him into her arms.

"Scratch me and you're off tuna for a month." Hilda raised a warning finger. "This won't hurt a bit."

"That's what the vet always says."

Zelda scowled. "I thought he agreed to try the potion of his own free will."

"I was blackmailed," Salem whined.

"Was he?" Zelda demanded, setting the beaker back on the rack.

"We told him there might be side effects and he made his own choice," Marigold said defensively.

"Some choice! Be a cookie jar with a ridiculous Cheshire grin or sacrifice myself to science."

"All right. So Marigold did apply a little pressure for incentive." Releasing the cat onto the labtop, Hilda looked at him pleadingly. "Would you do it for sautéed shrimp and scallops for dinner?"

Salem's whiskers twitched. "Every night for a week. With sushi on the side. I've had this lingering craving ever since I got booted out of the local sushi bar. Apparently, hard cash doesn't talk loud enough if you're a cat."

"Deal." Hilda extended her hand to shake.

Salem held up his paw and looked at Zelda. "What's the real lowdown on potential side effects?"

"All I can say for sure is that they wouldn't be permanent." Zelda stared at the beaker. "There's an even chance only one of two things will happen, though."

"I'm listening."

"Either nothing will happen or you'll get younger."

"Come on, Salem," Hilda coaxed. "Be a sport."

Impatient to see what *would* happen, Amanda pointed the deciding words into the cat's mouth.

"Okay, I'll do it." Salem gasped. "Wait! I didn't say that!"

"Yes, you did!" Escaped wisps of hair from

Marigold's french twist flared out from her head, and her eyes glinted with mad scientist delight.

Sighing, Salem nodded. "Make that all I can eat shrimp and scallops for a week and you've got a deal."

"Done." Jiggling with anticipation, Hilda motioned for Zelda to get on with it.

Hoping to see Salem reduced to boneless jelly or turned into a monstrous mutant, Amanda held her breath as Aunt Zelda carefully measured out an eye-dropper full of yellow goo and squeezed it into a saucer.

Salem took a tentative whiff and sneezed. "Phew! It smells like swamp water. Somebody hold my nose!"

"Sure." Aunt Hilda gently held a finger under the cat's nose as he lapped up the potion. When he finished, he sat back on his haunches and licked the last drops off his chin.

"Tastes better than it smells. A little like cod liver oil, I think."

"Nothing's happening." Marigold leaned closer to peer at the cat's face. "Do you feel anything?"

"Tingles, shivers, hot flashes?" Aunt Hilda asked hopefully.

"Younger?" Rubbing her chin, Zelda studied him intently.

"Nope. Can't say that I dooooooooo—"

Amanda slapped her hand over her mouth to keep from laughing out loud as the cat shrank with a whistling *whoosh.*

"Oops."

"Oops is hardly the word to describe this, Zelda." Stunned, Hilda grabbed the tiny black kitten Salem had become as he pounced on a stir stick beside the labtop.

"Well . . ." Zelda shrugged. "He got younger."

"This isn't the result I was hoping for," Marigold said with a disappointed sigh.

"Salem? Speak to me!" Hilda pleaded.

"Gah! Goo!"

Holding the little ball of fluff in front of her face, Hilda jerked as baby Salem batted her nose. "He's forgotten how to talk! Does that mean he's forgotten everything else, too?"

"Let me see him." Taking the kitten, Zelda looked him in the eye. "If you remember who you are, blink once."

"That routine is getting old." Sitting down, Hilda propped her chin in her hand. "And it looks like we're gonna be stuck getting old, too."

Marigold sank into the chair beside her. "Personally, I'd rather age gracefully then go through childhood again, especially if I won't remember anything."

"You won't remember anything." Setting the kitten on the floor, Zelda shook her head. "He's completely regressed back to his toddler days."

"I don't think Salem ever was a kitten, though," Hilda said. "After the verdict in his world domination trial, Drell turned him into a full-grown cat."

"Irrelevant," Zelda said. "Salem's a cat now and

not a warlock, so the formula reversed his feline aging process."

"But for how long?" Hilda asked. "I mean, does he have to grow up all over again, or is this a temporary condition?"

"I wasn't going for a temporary aging cure." Zelda winced as baby Salem leaped off the labtop and attacked the fringe on a throw rug. "I might be able to develop an antidote, but we'd better stock up on kitten food just in case."

Perfect. Amanda grinned. If her mother were a toddler, Arnie wouldn't stick around and Marigold couldn't send her away to boarding school. She just had to wait for the right moment to slip her a dose of the elixir.

Chapter 10

Sabrina removed the invisible blinders that blocked her peripheral vision and the earplugs with a quick point as she stepped off the bus. Her English teacher had let everyone work on their term papers during seventh period and the precautions probably hadn't been necessary, but she had gotten through the rest of the day without popping out. Now, she was only a short walk away from home and help.

Bursting through the front door, Sabrina almost tripped over a frolicsome black kitten chasing a spongy cat ball. "Salem? Is that you?"

"Grrrr!" Ignoring her, the kitten pounced, then scrambled after a catnip mouse as it shot out from under his paws.

"At least you're not a cookie jar any more." Sabrina's amusement at baby Salem's antics quickly faded as certain implications became apparent. Had Amanda somehow rigged the cookie jar spell so Marigold couldn't restore Salem to his former adult self? "Aunt Hilda! Aunt Zelda!"

"We're in here!" Aunt Zelda yelled back.

Dropping her parka, bag, and books on the sofa, Sabrina raced into the dining room. Aunt Zelda was hunched over the labtop, frowning with concentration. Sitting across from her, Cousin Marigold looked depressed, as though she had just been dropped from the Top Ten Best-Dressed Witches list.

"Where's Aunt Hilda?"

"Making some tuna puree for Salem," Aunt Zelda said absently, her gaze focused on an open spiral notebook.

"What happened to him anyway?" Dropping into another chair, Sabrina squealed as kitten claws latched onto the hem of her jeans.

"My latest scientific achievement seems to be Instant Kitten." Aunt Zelda sighed.

"Actually, Zelda discovered the secret of eternal youth," Marigold said dryly. "Except the formula works a tad too well."

"Great!"

Aunt Zelda glanced up curiously.

"I mean, I'm glad it wasn't something Amanda

did when she turned him into a cookie jar," Sabrina said.

"You knew about that?" Aunt Zelda asked. "Why didn't you tell us?"

"I left you a note on the bathroom mirror and I tried to call, but the line was busy. And I couldn't pop home because Amanda must have put a lockout clause in the random popping spell I've been dealing with all day."

"Slow down." Leaning back, Zelda held up a hand. "What random popping spell?"

Marigold withered with exasperation as Sabrina explained. "Don't worry, Sabrina. I'll pop her in and have her reverse it immediately."

"Can't you just do it, Marigold?" Sabrina really wasn't in the mood to see Amanda in person. Devious and cunning beyond her years, she'd find a way to make matters worse.

"Amanda has got to learn to take responsibility for her actions. There's no reason she shouldn't start *before* she gets to Miss Laura-Lye's boarding school tomorrow."

"You're sending her away to school?" Sabrina wasn't surprised that Marigold was finally taking some definitive disciplinary action, but she pitied the people who worked at the school. "Don't forget to attach a warning label. This child may be hazardous to your health. Contents may explode under pressure."

"Not necessary," Aunt Zelda said. "Compared

to Miss Laura-Lye, Sergeant Slater at Witch Camp is a teddy bear."

"Cool!" Sabrina nodded her approval as Marigold pointed up a TV programmed with Super Secret Insider Vision.

"Kitty, kitty, kitty!" Aunt Hilda poked her head through the kitchen door. "Hi, Sabrina! Where's Salem? His snack is ready and I want to make sure he's still litter-box trained."

"Climbing my leg!" Reaching under the table, Sabrina pulled the kitten off her jeans and held him out to Hilda. "I think I liked him better when he was an incorrigible adult."

"I think he's kind of cute. I've always regretted not getting Salem when he was a kitten." Cuddling the kitten, Hilda retreated back into the kitchen.

"Oh, dear." Drumming her fingers on the table, Marigold looked at Sabrina apologetically. "Amanda's not in her room."

"She's not?" Sabrina glanced at the Insider Vision screen—

Pingggg!

—Standing in the middle of Amanda's bedroom, Sabrina planted her hands on her hips. "This isn't a fairy tale! It's real! So why did I pop in here?"

No one answered.

Annoyed, but grateful that Amanda wasn't nearby, Sabrina wandered to the canopy bed to wait until she popped out again.

Dominated by pink ruffles and frills with white ribbon and lace accents, the room hardly reflected Amanda's personality. Everything from the stuffed animals arranged on the pillows to the books with color-coordinated bindings on the shelves was in perfect order, reminding Sabrina more of Marigold than her unruly daughter. She wondered how Amanda would decorate if left to her own devices.

"Early dungeon complete with rack and manacles no doubt." Sabrina sank onto the bed.

"Get up! Get up! Get up!"

"Okay! Okay! Okay!" As soon as Sabrina stood up the indentation she had made in the quilted comforter disappeared.

"Am I smooth again? Are the pillows still fluffed?" the bed asked frantically.

"You get an A-plus in wrinkle-free. I could bounce a quarter off you." Sabrina was no stranger to talking furniture. The talking living room pieces delivered to her house by mistake had been a surprise hit at her Halloween party.

"Thanks. I didn't mean to scare you, but I've got a severe case of rumple-phobia. Amanda will jump all over me and make me do fifty wrinkle-outs if I'm not perfect when she gets home."

Sabrina's heart went out to the nervous bed. "Then you'll be happy to know that as of tomorrow, Amanda will be vacating the premises for a while."

"You're not kidding, are you?"

"Witch's honor. Marigold's sending her to boarding school."

Suddenly, the room came alive with laughter, sobs of joy, and jubilant cheers. The bows on the ruffled curtains untied themselves and waved. The drawers in a highboy banged open and closed. Throw rugs took flight and swooped around the room. A huge smiley face appeared on the dressing table mirror, and the rousing strains of "Shout" recorded by Joey Dee and the Starlighters blared from the stereo.

"You know you make me want to shout!"

The talking furniture and the mirror joined in.

Sabrina clapped along as a coatrack pulled a bathrobe off one of its prongs and began to dance. The stuffed animals jumped up and down on the bed in time to the beat. A cane-backed desk chair do-si-doed with a floor lamp.

"Kick my heels up! Shout!"

When the shoes in the closet formed a conga line and headed for the door, Sabrina grabbed the knob to open it. A jolting electrical shock sizzled through her. Stunned, her immediate reaction was delayed a moment. "Ouch!"

The music stopped and everything quickly began putting itself back where it belonged.

Shaking the buzz from her head, Sabrina glanced in the mirror and squealed. Her long, silken hair looked as if it had been fried, curled with a corkscrew, then ordered to stand at attention. Supercharged with static, her turtleneck and jeans were plastered to her body. Wisps of smoke drifted from the sparking rivets on her jean pockets.

"I think you're a bit overdone, dear," the mirror said calmly.

"Fricasseed, frizzed, and frazzled," Sabrina groaned.

"I think the effect is rather spectacular." The bed carefully tucked in the corners of the sheets, then pulled the quilted comforter into place. "The beginning of a new fashion trend, perhaps!"

"Believe me, the KFC look will never catch on."

"Are my seams straight?" the bed asked.

Pinggg!

"Sabrina! Are you all right?" Aunt Zelda rushed to her side as she popped back in. "We saw the whole thing!"

"I'm fine. Considering that I look like a Frankenstein's bride wannabe!"

"Do something, Marigold," Zelda said firmly.

"That trap was meant for me." Numb, Marigold stared at the Insider Vision screen. "Amanda rigged that shock treatment for me!"

"But Sabrina got zapped instead. So please undo the damage, Marigold." Zelda stamped her foot. "Now!"

Marigold was oblivious. "My own daughter! Can you believe—"

"Fix Sabrina now or I'll report you to the ORSPCF!"

"The what?" Sabrina asked.

"The Other Realm Society for the Prevention of

Cruelty to Furniture. Amanda's sentient pieces have obviously been abused. If she wasn't leaving tomorrow, I'd zap them all to a used furniture shelter in a second."

Fuming, Marigold scowled. "If Amanda thinks I'll change my mind about boarding school now, she's got another thing—"

"Marigold!" Zelda shouted.

"Oh. Yes, of course." Sagging into a chair, Marigold casually pointed a fix-it spell.

When the tingling in her veins and the buzzing in her head subsided, Sabrina cautiously touched her hair. "Well?"

"All better." Zelda pointed, then held up the mirror that appeared in her hand.

"One Amanda malady cured and one to go." Double-checking to make sure no hair remained crimped, Sabrina turned to Marigold. "Have you found Amanda yet?"

"No." Marigold sighed. "I've got Insider-Net doing an Other Realm search, but so far—"

"We'll all be better off if you just reverse the popping spell, Marigold," Zelda said.

Taking a deep breath, Marigold nodded and began to chant.

"Amanda's magic spell now stopping.
Gone Sabrina's random popping."

Sabrina tensed as Marigold's finger flicked toward her. "I didn't feel anything."

"That's not unusual," Zelda assured her.

"Maybe, but I'd like to run a test to be sure. No offense, Marigold."

"None taken. Besides, the sooner we settle your problem, the sooner Zelda can get back to finding an antidote for her be-a-baby-again formula. And *then* maybe she can figure out what went wrong and fix it!"

Nothing like priorities, Sabrina thought.

Rolling her eyes, Zelda motioned Sabrina into the living room and picked up the remote.

"Wait!" Sabrina placed a restraining hand on Zelda's arm. "Just in case the spell hasn't been reversed, let's make sure I pop into something safe. No CNN, Animal Planet, or the Country Music Channel."

"Good thinking. Hilda was watching *Grease* on video last night. How's that?"

"Sure!" Sabrina nodded, realizing that present circumstances presented some intriguing possibilities. If Marigold *hadn't* reversed Amanda's spell, she could at least *choose* what she popped into this time. So why not grab the chance to dance with John Travolta? She'd just have to leave the room while Aunt Zelda set the tape. . . .

Zelda turned on the VCR, hit Play, then turned on the TV. "Here goes!"

"No! Wait!" Sabrina waved—

Pingggg!

"Look at me, I'm Sandra Dee, lousy with—"

Freezing her hand in mid wave, Sabrina smiled tightly as Rizzo turned away from the mirror and stopped singing to glare at her.

Good-bye, John. Hello, trouble.

☆

Chapter 11

☆

The distress Sabrina felt because she was still popping into TV screens was set aside in the face of a more immediate concern. She had popped into the *Grease* slumber party scene, and Rizzo, the tough, outspoken leader of the Pink Ladies, wasn't delighted to see her.

"Who invited you?" Rizzo asked.

Sabrina flinched. Even wearing a purple shirt and a ridiculous blond wig, Rizzo was intimidating. "Don't mind me. I'm just popping through."

Frenchy stared open-mouthed, then slapped her hands to a head full of hairpin curls covered with a turquoise hair net. "It's Sandra Dee! In person!"

"No, it's not." Rizzo paused to give Sabrina a rude once-over. "Are you?"

"Are you kidding?" Jan scoffed. Her dark ponytails bobbed as she waved to dismiss the absurd idea. "Sandra Dee would never wear that. That outfit is the *most!*"

"The most what?" Sabrina thought it was a compliment, but she wasn't sure.

"Keen? Hip? The opposite of square?" Hugging a plush panda and sitting on a bed covered with a flower-print bedspread, Marty shrugged. "Cool?"

"Oh! Right. Cool. I know that one." Nodding inanely, Sabrina looked from one suspicious face to another. "Thanks."

"Uh-huh." Folding her arms, Rizzo shifted her weight to one hip. "She's blond and dense, so maybe she is Sandra Dee."

Giggling, Frenchy scurried to a door marked Powder Room and knocked. "Sandy! Come on out! The *real* Sandra Dee is here! In *my* bedroom!"

Squinting intently, Jan leaned forward. "Nope. Her ears are pierced."

Annoyed at being scrutinized like a badly dressed mannequin in a display window, Sabrina adopted a similar disdainful attitude. "Actually, I'm Sabrina."

"What kind of a name is that? Sa-bree-na." Looking thoroughly disgusted, Rizzo flopped on the bed. "Isn't that some kind of fancy French cheese?"

"Maybe it's a cheerleader name?" Frenchy suggested.

"I've never *met* a cheerleader who could utter a

snide remark." A sly grin spread across Rizzo's face. "But if I ever did meet one—"

"That's a rumble I wouldn't want to miss," Marty said.

Sabrina raised her pointing finger, envisioning a verbal duel between Libby and the rough-and-ready Pink Lady. "One of these days, have I got a treat for you."

"Sounds like Sandy's still sick. Maybe I'd better leave her alone until she gets over it." Easing away from the bathroom door, Frenchy smiled. "Want to sleep over with us, Sabrina?"

"Frenchy! You have to stop making friends with every stray nobody that drops in out of nowhere!"

"No, I don't, Rizzo. I like Sandy, and Sabrina looks lost." The perky soon-to-be-beauty-school-dropout stood firm. "It's my house, so she can stay."

"All right." Rizzo reluctantly gave in, but not without having the last word. "But only if she's not a party pooper like the Goody Two-shoes in the bathroom."

"No, I'm more of a party popper. In fact, I'll probably be popping out again real soon."

Please, Sabrina wished, wondering why fate couldn't have zapped her into the televised dance at Rydell High or the graduation carnival scene instead of tossing her into the middle of girls' night out with the catty and crass.

"As long as you're here, have a seat." Standing up, Rizzo directed Sabrina to the bed and straightened the blond wig on her head. "Okay. Where was I?"

Marty, Frenchy, and Jan shrugged.

"'Look at me, I'm Sandra Dee—'" Sabrina recited the lyric. "'Lousy with—'"

"Oh, yeah. One of my two big numbers." Stepping to the mirror, Rizzo threw out her arms and sang. "'Look at me, I'm Sandra—'"

Sabrina sighed, recalling her spontaneous rendition of "Oh, What a Beautiful Morning." So far, that had been the high point of the day—

Pinggg!

Shaking off the dizziness, Sabrina collapsed on the sofa.

Turning off the TV, Zelda dropped down beside her. "Something is dreadfully wrong here."

"Yeah, Aunt Hilda's timing for one." Sabrina exhaled wearily. "She could have stopped the tape in one of the cool parts with John Travolta."

"Why didn't Marigold's reversal spell work?" Zelda muttered, mystified. "Are you absolutely *positive* Amanda put the spell on you, Sabrina?"

"Who else?"

"You've got a point." Rising, Zelda patted Sabrina's shoulder. "Maybe Marigold can shed some light on this. Coming?"

Sabrina shook her head. "After I catch my breath, I think I'll go wait in my room. No books. No TV. No pop."

"Try not to worry. I'll call you when we figure this out."

If you figure it out.

Letting her head fall back, Sabrina closed her eyes. If she was smart, she'd go to straight to bed and sleep until the crisis was over.

Safely camouflaged in the photograph on the wall, Amanda elevated the dropper loaded with youth potion when Zelda came back into the dining room. Her mother set down her glass of club soda with lemon when she and Hilda turned to look, giving her the opening she had been waiting for.

"What's wrong, Zelda?" Hilda asked.

As Amanda slowly moved the dropper toward her mother's glass, she inhaled sharply. Baby Salem was on the floor, crouched and ready to pounce, his gaze fastened on the enticing object floating above the table.

"Please, don't tell us there's no way to correct the formula."

"It's not the *formula* I'm worried about right now, Marigold." Zelda sat down.

Carefully lowering the dropper to the labtop, Amanda turned her finger toward a wadded-up sheet of notebook paper under Zelda's chair. *Flick!* The paper twitched, snagging the kitten's attention. *Flick!* Salem bounded after the paper as it scooted across the floor.

"What was that?" Lifting her shoeless feet, Marigold frantically scanned the floor.

Amanda lifted the dropper again, glad that she

had inherited her father's nerves of steel and unwavering commitment to purpose. If she were as skittish and neurotic as Marigold, she'd never get away with anything.

"It's just Salem playing with Zelda's discarded notes."

Pointing ever so carefully, Amanda moved the dropper into position and lowered it into her mother's glass until the tip barely touched the clear liquid.

"So what's the matter?" Hilda asked again.

Zelda held up her hands, indicating she needed a moment to think.

Hilda and Marigold looked at each other.

Amanda held her breath and the dropper steady. The instant both women shifted their attention back to Zelda, she squeezed the rubber bulb. A dark yellow streak of potion shot through the carbonated soda.

Yes!

And a high-pitched banshee shriek shattered the anxious silence.

"Now what?" Marigold threw up her hands.

Amanda smothered her giggles with her hand. The mostly boring day was about to get very interesting.

"Sabrina!" Zelda's chair fell over as she stood up.

"What about Sabrina?" Hilda asked, worried.

"Stay here, Hilda, and make sure Salem doesn't

disturb *anything* on the labtop. Marigold! You're with me."

"Since when are you giving me orders, Zelda?"

"Since your daughter invaded our home and decided to have a little fun at our expense. Let's go!" Eyes and finger flashing, Zelda popped upstairs.

Hilda glared at Marigold. "If you want to see another birthday, go with her."

Marigold went.

Rats. Disappointed because her mother had gotten a momentary reprieve from second childhood, Amanda faded into the background of the photograph to await further developments.

Rising, Hilda stared at the ceiling and paced. "I hate it when disaster strikes and I don't have a hint about what's going on. And I can never remember an X-ray vision spell when I need one." She stopped pacing abruptly. "And I'm babbling to myself."

"Gah!" Salem raced back into the room, took a flying leap onto the table, and slid into Hilda's glass of club soda, tipping it over.

"Thanks a lot, Salem. Tragedy is stalking the house. This is no time to be fooling around." A quick point removed the broken glass and puddle.

Perched on the corner of the table, Salem blinked at her with kitten innocence, then began to groom himself.

"Not so close to the labtop, Salem. Get down."

Salem didn't budge except to rub his face with his freshly licked paw.

"Shoo!" Giving the kitten a gentle push, Hilda dropped into Marigold's vacated chair as he scampered off to nurse his wounded feline dignity. "Makes me wonder why people keep cats that don't understand a word they say. Then again, why would that matter? Salem hardly ever listens."

Glancing at the ceiling, Hilda sighed and reached for Marigold's drink.

Amanda leaned forward expectantly. She didn't know whether to laugh or cry when Hilda drained the glass.

Sabrina was standing in the hall, staring through her bedroom door when Zelda and Marigold popped to the rescue. "Someone turned my room into a home for the Swamp"—her hand flew to her mouth before the word *Thing* triggered another popping episode—"monster."

Stunned, Zelda couldn't say anything for a moment.

Marigold wrinkled her nose. "It's uh, incredibly realistic, isn't it?"

"For a house swamp." Sabrina sagged. Two feet of putrid water formed a wall across the door, confining the swamp to her room. Gnarled trees and tangled brush grew in profusion around the perimeter, and eerie animal sounds rose from the pervasive gloom. An owl sitting on the headboard of her drifting bed hooted, and a frog emerged from a muddy bank in the far corner.

"Amanda." Zelda said simply.

"How could she do this?" Marigold asked. "Hilda sent her back to the Other Realm."

"Since when does Amanda stay put because an adult tells her to?" Zelda countered accusingly.

"Maybe *he* knows." Sabrina pointed to the frog that was swimming as fast as it could kick across the surface of the water. Climbing onto a partially submerged log near the door, it leaped into the V of Marigold's jacket and hooked its front legs in the fabric to hang on.

Marigold was instantly reduced to blithering hysterics. "Get it off me! Get it off!"

"Rivet, rivet, rivet!"

"That doesn't look like normal frog behavior to me, Aunt Zelda."

"Get it off!" Screeching, Marigold bounced up and down.

The frog stuck. "Rivet, rivet, rivet!"

"Could be it's not really a frog," Zelda said.

"My thoughts exactly." Gently placing her hands around the slick green amphibian, Sabrina removed it.

Marigold covered her face with her hands and sobbed.

Sabrina sighed. Considering that Marigold hadn't seen Amanda all day, she was a pitiful mess. Strands of hair hung limply around her head. A toe popped out of a run in her stocking, and her white linen jacket had muddy frog prints all over it. Her makeup smeared as she collected herself and wiped her eyes.

"Rivet! Rivet!"

"Did Amanda turn whoever you are into a frog?" Sabrina asked.

The frog nodded.

"Marigold," Zelda said gently. "Remove the spell on the frog and we'll get some answers."

Nodding, Marigold sniffled as she pointed to the frog Sabrina placed on the floor.

"Denizen of Sabrina's bog,
Be what you are and not a frog."

The frog transformed into a chubby little man with glasses and a thick head of white hair. He was wearing a white shirt with old-fashioned gartered sleeves and a shopkeeper's apron.

"Gerald!" Zelda looked shocked.

"Gerald?" Sabrina had never met the man.

"The owner of Precious Powders, Limited." Pale and shaken, Marigold nervously wrung her hands. "It's an exclusive shop that sells all the gourmet spell ingredients that are so hard to find these days."

"Everyone thought you were away on another rare fungus safari, Gerald." Zelda frowned. "Who would dare turn the Other Realm's foremost expert on mushrooms, fungi, and spore extracts into a frog?"

"Don't I wish that was the sixty-four-thousand-dollar question," Sabrina muttered.

"Don't forget toadstools, lichen, and molds." Gerald cleaned his glasses with the hem of his apron, then held them up to the light. "And to answer your question, Amanda did."

"Why?" Marigold asked, aghast.

Sabrina suspected she was not mortified because of Amanda's bad behavior, but afraid Gerald would cut off her supply of rare herbs and spell spices.

"Because I refused to sell her pulverized liverwort spores, a commodity that is strictly regulated by the Witches All-Natural Substances Authority and forbidden to unlicensed witches under the age of eighteen."

"I'm allergic to liverwort spore!" Marigold gasped. "It makes my vocal cords seize up so I can't talk and lowers my body temperature so I can hardly move."

"There's a thought to brighten a dreary day." Zelda smiled wistfully.

"Apparently, Amanda thought so, too," Sabrina said.

Gerald shoved his glasses back on, then peered at Marigold over the rim. "Amanda didn't even give me a chance to explain! I said 'no' and then I was a frog! I've never seen such a fast finger on a child."

"You didn't know Hilda when she was a kid," Zelda said.

"I am *so* sorry, Gerald." Marigold humbled

herself with an apologetic smile that could have been mistaken for a pained grimace. "If there's anything I can do to make it up to you, anything at all . . ."

Sabrina arched an eyebrow, expecting Marigold to fall on her knees and crawl.

"Unfortunately, there's no factory recall on defective children. So since you're Amanda's mother, you're responsible. Until she apologizes to me and makes reasonable restitution, you are no longer a preferred customer, Marigold. You are *banned* from my store!"

"But—but—but—"

"Good day, ladies, and thank you." With a curt bow to Zelda and Sabrina, Gerald ran for the linen closet.

"Wait a minute!" Sabrina called. "How'd you end up in my room? And how did my room end up a swamp?"

"Amanda brought me along because she thought I'd enjoy a nice wallow in the mud!" Gerald slammed the closet door behind him.

"But—but—but—" Marigold stuttered.

Zelda grabbed Marigold's arms and shook her. "Snap out of it! Amanda's back in the mortal world somewhere, and we've got to find her!"

"Yeah!" Sabrina said adamantly. "I'm not sharing my room with an alligator, and I've definitely had enough interactive TV for one day."

Marigold nodded with a shuddering sob. "But I don't make a habit of lingering in the mortal world any longer than necessary, so I don't know where she might have gone!"

"You must have some idea, Marigold," Zelda insisted.

The ear-piercing wail of an enraged child reverberated through the floor.

"Downstairs?" Marigold said.

The Quizmaster's questions should be so easy to answer, Sabrina thought as she popped into the dining room behind Zelda and Marigold. However, she was not at all prepared for what they found.

Amanda was holding baby Salem out of the reach of a girl toddler with blond curls who was bawling and wearing a "Witchfest '76" T-shirt that was several sizes too big.

"Aunt Hilda?"

☆

Chapter 12

☆

Pointing at Salem with one hand and rubbing her eye with the other, baby Hilda stopped crying long enough to squeal. "Wan kee! Wan kee!"

Staring at little Hilda with astonished disbelief, Zelda faltered. "I think she wants the kitty."

"How old is she?" Sabrina asked, trying not to laugh.

Zelda shrugged. "Two? and a half?"

"It serves her right," Marigold said, her tone totally lacking in sympathy. "She knew that youth potion would make her a lot younger than she wanted to be. And she took it anyway."

"She also knew I might not be able to make an antidote. So there's no way she would have taken it." Zelda looked at Amanda. "Not *deliberately.*"

Confronted with two mind-boggling shocks in less than ten minutes, swamp room and toddler aunt, Sabrina had forgotten that the pint-size perpetrator had finally been tracked down. However, her furious attention was diverted from Amanda by the cries of the other incorrigible child in the room.

"Wan' kee! Wan' kee!" Hiccuping and sniveling, baby Hilda pressed her demand with a foot-stamping fit.

"How about a lollipop and some nice, new clothes instead?" Pointing up a cherry lollipop, Sabrina held it out with a smile. "I sure hope you're potty trained."

"Stinky," Hilda said as she reached for the candy.

"Definitely two," Zelda stated flatly.

A sharp look from Marigold silenced Amanda's giggles.

"Eew! Ripe!" Catching a whiff, Sabrina executed another quick flick, changing little Hilda into a clean diaper, a white T-shirt, and pink corduroy rompers with a quilted bunny on the bib. "I don't think I've ever appreciated my magic finger more."

"Wan pop!" Scowling, Hilda pursed her lips in a pout.

"Anything to avoid another tantrum." Muttering through gritted teeth, Sabrina gave her the promised treat.

"Sanks, Breena." Pacified for the moment, Hilda climbed onto a chair and smiled.

Sabrina blinked. No one had warned her that little kids were armed with some high-powered ammunition called cuteness and adorability. *With the exception of Amanda,* she thought, noticing Aunt Zelda's face.

"You did this to Hilda, didn't you, Amanda?" Seething with suppressed rage, Zelda took a step forward.

"I'll handle this." Holding Zelda off with a stern glance, Marigold squared her shoulders, folded her arms and switched into mad mother mode. "What did you do?"

"A lot of things, actually," Amanda said calmly. "I've been using my imagination just like you said I should."

"I noticed." Marigold fumed. "Did you deliberately give Hilda the youth potion?"

"Deliberately?" Amanda shook her head and switched Salem into her other arm. "No. It wasn't my fault Salem spilled her soda and she drank yours."

"Mine? You put the youth potion in *my* glass? *Knowing* it would turn me into a baby? How could you even *think* of doing such a despicable thing?"

"How could *you* decide to send *me* away to boarding school?"

Another easy question, Sabrina thought, but not one the stressed mother had the energy to answer. Overloading, Marigold fell into the nearest chair.

"How did you know about the formula, Amanda?" Zelda asked.

"Easy. After I left Sabrina's room, I popped into that picture up there. I heard everything you said."

Sabrina stared at the old family photograph on the wall. It was one of those unremarkable things a person stopped noticing after a while because it was always there. However, she was sure the people standing or sitting on chairs in front of the old colonial house hadn't looked quite so bedraggled and exhausted before. No one was smiling.

"Doesn't making people miserable ever get boring?" Sabrina didn't try to disguise her contempt.

"Nope." Amanda's serene expression betrayed not a hint of remorse as she scratched Salem behind the ears.

"Give me my cat!" Pulling the kitten out of the girl's arms, Sabrina retreated to the far side of the table. "And clean up my room."

"I don't want to. It's my decorating masterpiece!" Lifting her chin, Amanda stubbornly dared someone to make her.

"Are you sure about that?" Stone-faced with resolve, Marigold addressed her daughter with that totally calm and even tone all parents use when they reach their tolerance limit.

Sabrina smirked. She couldn't help herself. All kids recognized that *voice* and knew it meant they were in big trouble with no way out.

Amanda cringed slightly, but remained defiant. "Yes. The Midnight Swamp motif is the biggest and best terrarium I've ever made and I like it."

"Do you? Good thing." Marigold looked back at

Sabrina. "Since no swamp motif is complete without a frog and we sent Gerald back to the Other Realm, you can have Amanda."

Sabrina was about to protest, then realized that Marigold was setting up an ultimatum. "Really? Thanks. I've always wanted to turn someone into a frog." She pointed her finger at the stricken girl. "And I'm so glad it's going to be you."

"Mother! You can't be serious."

"Oh, I'm very serious. One way or another you're going to learn some manners and to respect the rights of others, Amanda." Marigold shrugged indifferently. "It doesn't matter to me if you learn it by living as a frog in Sabrina's swamp or at Miss Laura-Lye's boarding school."

Little Hilda burped. "'Scuse me."

"You're excused." Zelda covered an amused smile with her hand.

"So I have a choice?" Amanda asked cautiously.

Nodding, Marigold stood up and outlined the deal. Terms: nonnegotiable. "Option number one. You can be a frog and stay in the swamp until Sabrina releases you. Of course, you'll have to take your chances with the other inhabitants."

Tired of being held, Salem squirmed in Sabrina's arms and she set him on the floor. Amanda was squirming, too, but she wasn't going to get off so easily.

Amanda sighed. "What's the second option?"

"You will cease and desist your pranks as of right now. You will put Sabrina's room back the way it was—and I mean *exactly* the way it was." Anger seeped into Marigold's quickening speech. "And you will go to Miss Laura-Lye's boarding school and stay there until you graduate! And I don't care if that takes a hundred years!"

Amanda frowned, as though she had to think about which option to chose.

"And she has to reverse the popping into books and TV spell," Sabrina said.

"That, too." Marigold glared at her daughter, waiting for an answer.

"What popping spell?" Amanda looked genuinely perplexed.

"You know what spell!" Sabrina paused until her rush of unleashed fury and frustration passed. "The one you put on me so I'd pop into any book or TV show I saw or heard mentioned. The one that wouldn't let me pop back home?"

"Oohhh! *That* spell. I didn't cast that one." Amanda smiled and pointed at Hilda. "She did."

Hilda looked up and wiped cherry lollipop goo off her mouth with her arm.

"Run that by me one more time, Aunt Zelda." Pacing by the labtop, Sabrina glanced at the ceiling. Marigold and Amanda were upstairs undoing the swamp spells on her room.

"I just explained it, Sabrina." Pulling her chair up to the table, Zelda typed a command into her portable computer.

"I know, but I just want to be sure I understand

why I may have to spend the next ten or twelve years avoiding TV and novels. Unless I'm in the mood for a trashy romance or a high-speed car chase through the streets of L.A."

"It's very simple. Aunt Hilda cast the spell to get rid of Amanda. Let's see—how did Amanda say it went?"

Sabrina recited the spell in a monotone. "'Witches pop in and out in books and TV, but you can't pop in here whenever you please.' Or something like that."

"That sounds right." Zelda nodded, then shook a frantic arm as little Hilda stood on the chair and reached for a test tube. "Hilda! No! Don't touch anything! You have sticky stuff all over your fingers!"

Hilda's little face contorted.

Recognizing the warning signs of a crying jag, Sabrina pointed up a box of assorted toys and a plastic container of wet-wipes. "It's okay, Hilda. First we'll wash your hands and then you can play."

"Yuck!" Hilda turned her sticky face to avoid the wet-wipe in Sabrina's hand. "No!"

"Yes!" Persevering, Sabrina managed to clean most of the candy residue off Hilda's face and hands. Then she set the petulant child on the floor. "Go play."

"That should last all of five minutes," Zelda muttered.

"We can hope." Pushing her hair behind her

ears, Sabrina sat down. "The popping spell, Aunt Zelda."

"Oh, yes." Taking a deep breath, Zelda launched into a step-by-step explanation of events as she thought they had happened. "Hilda chanted the spell and pointed, but Amanda ducked."

"Just as I stepped out of my room. So it hit me."

"But not directly," Zelda said. "I'm pretty sure you stepped out a split second after the spell went by. You were zapped when it ricocheted off the hall mirror."

Sabrina nodded, remembering that she *had* stepped into the hall to look in the mirror before popping out to school. "But what difference would that make?"

Pointing up a cup of herbal tea, Zelda took a sip. "Bouncing off the mirror altered Hilda's general statement about how witch popping is portrayed in TV shows and books and made it the emphasis of the spell rather than a throwaway rhyming line."

"I don't get it."

Sighing, Zelda put the cup down and clasped her hands. "Hilda said 'pop in and out *in* books and TV,' but the ricochet effect changed '*in* books' to '*of* books.' "

. . . pop in and out of *books . . .*

Running the phrase through her mind suddenly made everything clear. Sabrina sat back, amazed at the drastic difference one little word could make. She also realized that the second line had been the original focus of Hilda's spell: to prevent Amanda from dropping into the Spellman house uninvited whenever she felt like it. That line had also prevented *her* from popping home. The busy phone line had been a bizarre fluke. According to Aunt Zelda, Aunt Hilda had deliberately blocked incoming calls so the youth potion project wouldn't be interrupted by sales pitches, wrong numbers, or surveys.

Surveys! She had promised to meet Val after school to decide on a fix for the "Students Speak" column! The nervous editor was probably trying to call her right now. *Good thing the line's still busy,* Sabrina thought grimly. Until she stopped popping, she was confined to quarters.

And reversing the random popping spell had become a more difficult, if not impossible, problem.

The problem toddled over to Zelda with a plastic bucket in her hand. "Wha's this?"

Zelda pulled the lid off. "Little plastic blocks you snap together to make things."

Hilda pulled out a green block. "Wha's this?"

"A green block!" Worried and losing patience, Sabrina snapped and immediately regretted it.

Hilda's mouth puckered.

Zelda quickly pulled two blocks out of the bucket and snapped them together. "This is how you do it. See?"

"Do 'gain."

"No, you do 'gain. Again." Smiling with effort, Zelda patted Hilda's head. "Go play."

Hilda walked two steps, dumped the bucket of blocks, then sat down to rummage through them.

"That noise makes it so hard to think." Zelda massaged her forehead.

"Try," Sabrina pleaded. "There's got to be some way we can get Hilda to reverse the spell."

"Not in her present condition there isn't." Zelda watched Hilda snapping blocks together with no particular shape or color scheme in mind. "Her vocabulary is too limited, and she wouldn't understand what we wanted her to do. And *that* could just make a bad situation worse."

"There's a scary thought." An image of living with the Brady Bunch or hanging out with Laverne and Shirley until Hilda was old enough to retrieve her flashed through Sabrina's mind. "I think I'll take my chances with things as they are."

"Well, don't give up hope." Straightening her paper notes, Zelda picked up a pen. "All I have to do is find an antidote for the youth potion. Then the Rugrat Hilda will be her old irascible, grown-up self and everything will be fine."

"In the meantime, I think I'll just lock myself in my room." Sabrina looked upward again. "After Amanda and Marigold are done draining it."

The plastic blocks scattered as the kitten Salem dove into the middle of the pile.

"No, kee! Go 'way!" Hilda shrieked, then shoved him aside and pointed.

Salem froze, crouched for another assault.

"Hilda!" Sabrina yelled.

Zelda casually glanced at the immobile kitten. "Hilda always was quick on the finger as a child. She was a hundred and sixteen before she finally learned to think before pointing."

"Aunt Zelda! She just turned Salem into a fuzzy statue!"

"Baby wish magic. Terribly annoying, but the effects aren't permanent."

"Are we talking minutes? Hours? Days?"

"It varies." Zelda's Witch-Bert screen saver disappeared as she moved the roller ball to call up her computer notes.

"Best guess, how long do you think finding the antidote will take?" Sabrina asked. "I'm supposed to meet Harvey at the roller rink tonight."

"Best guess, a lot longer if you keep asking me questions."

"Wha-cha doin', Delda?"

"Trying to work, Hilda. Which is almost impossible with an inquisitive audience. Which I've had to cope with all day." Zelda smiled tightly at the tot standing by her chair, then at Sabrina. "How badly do you want to make that date with Harvey tonight?"

Taking the hint, Sabrina stood up. "I'll take her into the kitchen and make her a snack. Chocolate cake should keep her happy for a while."

"Cake! Wan' cake!" Laughing, Hilda clapped her hands.

"I'm not sure she'll thank you for the extra calories when she gets back to normal, Sabrina."

"But she couldn't have a better excuse for indulging!" Tucking stiff Salem under one arm, Sabrina took Hilda's hand. "I've got to work on the survey column Val and I are doing for the *Lantern* anyway. I should give her a call—"

"Can't," Zelda said. "Hilda put a spell on the phone and the line's still busy."

"No phone!" Sabrina stomped through the kitchen doorway. "You know, Hilda, I'd hate to see what would happen if you *deliberately* set out to ruin someone's day."

Chapter 13

Sabrina glanced at the clock as she tried to clean chocolate icing with mashed cake crumbs off Hilda's face, hands, coveralls, the tablecloth, and the back of the chair. Salem, who had snapped out of Hilda's wish spell a few minutes ago, was taking care of the mess on the floor.

Only five o'clock?

The half hour she had spent watching Hilda attack and destroy two pieces of cake seemed a lot longer.

"Wan' down, Breena!" Hilda tried to wriggle out of the hold Sabrina had on her arm.

"Not until you're cleaned up." Reaching for another wet-wipe, Sabrina changed her mind and pointed instead. Icing and crumbs vanished from child, furniture, and floor, and her respect for mortal mothers rose by several degrees. Given how exasperating small children could be, it was hard to believe the world was in danger of overpopulation.

"Grrrr! Gah!" Irritated by the loss of his treat, Salem pounced on Sabrina's leg.

"Ouch! Stop that!" The back doorbell rang as Sabrina tried to shake the clinging kitten off her jeans. His claws dug deeper into the fabric.

"Wan' down!"

Lifting Hilda out of the booster seat on the chair, Sabrina reached for Salem as someone rang the bell again, then knocked.

Hilda wandered to the counter, opened the lower cabinet door and began dragging out the pots, pans, and cauldrons.

Harvey called out. "Hey, Sabrina!"

What's Harvey doing here? "Just a minute!"

"Hurry up, Sabrina! It's freezing out here!"

Val, too?

More frazzled now than when Amanda's doorknob had shocked her, Sabrina slipped into super-fast magic gear. Pointing up another box of toys, she dragged Hilda out of the cabinet and sat her on the floor. Flinging the pots, pans, and cauldrons back into the cabinet with another flick of her finger, she hobbled to the door with Salem's claws still imbedded in her leg.

"My lips are turning blue!" Val cried. Shivering, Harvey and Val both dashed inside as Sabrina flung the door open and quickly closed it behind them.

"Hi! What are you two doing here?"

"Your phone's out of order," Harvey said.

"No, I meant why didn't you go to the front door?"

Harvey shrugged. "We did. You didn't answer the front door. The bell must be out of order or something."

Val looked at her sternly. "We were supposed to get together after school to talk about the 'Students Speak' column, remember?"

"Uh, gosh, Val! I forgot. Something came up. An emergency and—"

"Another emergency or the same emergency you had at lunch?" Val started slipping out of her coat.

"No! You can't stay! It's, uh, a family emergency thing. Weird relatives and stuff."

"There's a kitten on your leg," Harvey said matter-of-factly.

Sabrina grabbed Salem to pull him off, but he held fast. "He's very attached to me."

"So I see." Val nodded. "Who's the kid?"

"Uh . . . the emergency! I, uh, had to rush home to baby-sit so my aunts could deal with a sensitive family problem."

"I hope it's nothing too serious?" Harvey frowned.

"A little swamp water, a runaway cousin, and an age-related crisis. Nothing to worry about."

"Watch TV 'toons, Breena." Hilda tugged on Sabrina's pants. "TV 'toons, peas."

"Hey, she's a cutie." Harvey grinned. "She kinda looks like your Aunt Hilda."

"Yeah, she does, doesn't she?" Sabrina laughed nervously, scooping up Hilda. The last thing she needed was to pop out in front of Harvey and Val for a romp through animation land with a bunch of zany talking animals. She wasn't anxious to plunge off a high cliff and emerge from a crater with only a gigantic throbbing bump on her head, either. As it was, she was barely hanging on to her sanity. Cartoon music alone would push her over the edge.

" 'Toons, Breena!"

"There aren't any 'toons on right now, Hilda."

"Yes, there are, Sabrina," Harvey said helpfully. "There's some really cool cartoon shows on in the afternoon. My little brother watches them all the time."

" 'Toons! 'Toons! 'Toons!" Hilda bounced up and down in Sabrina's arms.

"Thanks, Harvey. I'll remember that." Sabrina pried Hilda's fingers out of her hair. "I hate to be rude, but I've really got to give Hil—Heidi my full attention."

"She does seem a little spoiled." Val scowled with disapproval.

Grabbing Hilda's hand as she pointed her chubby wish finger at Val, Sabrina herded her two friends back to the door.

"What about our column, Sabrina?"

"Well, actually, I, uh . . . thought we could . . .

rephrase the question!" *Might work,* Sabrina thought. "How about 'Why *shouldn't* we make it socially acceptable for girls to ask boys out?' Then we can use all the answers we've already got in a general report that doesn't identify anyone."

"Not bad!" Grinning, Val backed out through the door Harvey held open. "Maybe I'll hit the mall and see if I can't get some better material to work with. Hope they fix your phone soon."

"Oh, so do I." Sabrina nodded. "You don't know how much."

Hilda yanked free of Sabrina's hand and darted away.

Harvey paused in the open doorway. "Are you gonna be done baby-sitting in time to go roller-skating?"

"I should be. But if I'm a little late, don't worry, okay?"

"Okay. See ya later!"

Sagging against the door after she closed it, Sabrina heaved a long, weary sigh. She wasn't at all sure she'd have the energy to roll when and if she got to the rink. Keeping Hilda entertained after spending the day popping in and out of tiring book and TV scenarios was sapping the last of her strength.

" 'Toons! Yay!" Hilda clapped. "A-B-C!"

Sabrina gasped when she looked and saw a wish-conjured TV on the floor in front of the little girl. Fortunately, Hilda wasn't tuned into a cartoon channel.

She was watching a local production called *Diggety Dan's Doghouse*—

Pingggg!

"Hey, boys and girls!" Wearing a white-and-black spotted dog costume with whiskers and a black nose painted on his face, Diggety Dan turned to the camera and clapped his paws. "Do you know what time it is?"

Time to hide!

Sabrina was standing under a fake tree on green carpet by a white picket fence with Dan's trained dog troop. Unfamiliar with dogs, she had no idea what was going on in the canine minds behind the four pairs of brown eyes staring at her.

"Nice doggies." Tentatively reaching out to let the large Old English sheepdog sniff her hand, she quickly withdrew it when a small terrier with wiry hair growled softly. A medium-size collie mix and a small poodle inched closer, noses twitching and ears perked forward.

"It's time to take a deep breath—" Diggety Dan drew in a long breath.

Sabrina suddenly realized baby Salem was still clinging to her jeans.

"And count to five! Ruff!" Dan opened his arms wide, then donned an exaggerated, puzzled expression. "But what will we count?"

And Salem suddenly realized he was surrounded by dogs.

"I know!" Dan squealed joyously. "Let's count fingers!"

"Yeow!" Kitten claws dug into Sabrina's leg as Salem scrambled to the safety of her shoulder.

"Ready? One—" The three smaller dogs began barking, drawing Diggety Dan's startled attention. The large sheepdog just sat.

"What the—"

Wincing, Sabrina tried to pull Salem's claws out of her turtleneck so she could hold him in her arms. Too panicked to understand, the kitten launched himself from her shoulder into the fake tree.

Still barking, the three dogs began leaping around the tree trunk. The sheepdog yawned.

"Sit!" Dan ordered, trying to restore order.

The dogs immediately stopped barking and sat.

"Salem!" Sabrina hissed. "Get down here!"

Cowering on a branch and partially hidden by plastic leaves, Salem paid no attention to her. His gaze was fastened on the canine threat sitting below him.

"Look who's here, everyone!" Glaring at Sabrina, the performer kept his voice light and cheery as he ambled over on flapping dog feet. "We have a surprise guest!"

Smiling tightly, Sabrina waved.

"Who are you, surprise guest?" Dan asked.

"Sa—" Giving her real name seemed like a bad idea, especially since this was a local show and Dan might decide to track her down. She doubted anyone she knew besides Hilda was watching, but why take a chance? "—mantha."

"And what are you doing here, Samantha?" Dan asked, his voice strained.

"My kitten's up in your tree!" Adopting Dan's kiddie-host singsong lilt, Sabrina made an effort to fit in. It wasn't Diggety Dan's fault she had popped in unannounced, and she didn't want to ruin his show totally.

"He is?" Clamping his padded costume paws to his face, Dan gasped. "Then we'd better get him down! Before he falls and hurts himself."

"That's a good idea, Diggety Dan!" Keeping a perky smile plastered on her face, Sabrina nodded vigorously.

Dan looked into the camera, speaking solemnly to his television audience at home. "Never, never climb trees unless someone is with you. Or *you* could fall and get very, very hurt."

"That's very, very good advice, Diggety Dan."

Taller than Sabrina, Dan reached up to grab Salem.

The little terrier barked.

Hissing, Salem swatted at the man-dog's paw.

"I don't think he wants to come down."

"But we have to go home soon!" Sabrina whined with a sad frown, then reverted to her phony smile again. She *did* have to get Salem back before she popped out. The kitten wasn't under Hilda's spell and she didn't know if he'd be trapped in the show. Anything was possible with magic gone awry. "I know!"

"What?" Dan asked sharply, losing patience.

"I'll use my magic finger to get him down!"

"That I'd like to see." Dan muttered, then brightened for the benefit of his young viewers. "That would be ter-*ruff*-ic! Wouldn't it, kids?"

To emphasize the point, Dan cued the dogs with a hand signal. The sheepdog continued to sit while the other three chased their tails in a circle around him. After a few seconds, they sat and barked once.

Running out of time before she vanished from the *Doghouse* set, Sabrina pointed up a cloud of blue smoke to camouflage Salem's instantaneous shift from the branch into her arms. A second point transferred the kitten.

Dan's face lit up with enthusiasm when the smoke cleared. "Look at that! Samantha has her kitten back!"

"Ta-da!" Sabrina raised one arm.

"How'd you do that?" Dan asked, intrigued.

Sabrina whispered. "He jumped."

Nodding, Dan segued back into the normal routine. "And now that Samantha's kitty is safely out of the tree, it's time to count to five!"

Obeying another hand signal, the four dogs lined up to Sabrina's right, making her number five. Dan began counting.

"One, two, three, four—"

Pinggg!

"Fi—Where'd she go?" Dan's voice rang from the TV speakers in the Spellman kitchen. "That was great!"

Hugging Salem to her chest, Sabrina closed her eyes until the momentary dizziness passed.

"Old Diggety Dan will have to get Samantha back real soon, hey—"

Hilda's wish TV disappeared.

And so had Hilda, Sabrina realized with a quick glance around the kitchen. Setting Salem on the counter, she looked between the island and the wall counter and inside the cabinets.

"Hilda!" Aunt Zelda said crossly. "I said, 'Don't touch!' "

Found her.

"Pretty bottle."

Sabrina dashed into the dining room as Hilda reached for a test tube full of iridescent blue jelly.

"Don't touch!" Aunt Zelda pushed her hand away. "That's mine and it's not a toy."

Before Sabrina or her aunt could act, Hilda pointed.

"Mine!"

Sabrina staggered as Aunt Zelda suddenly became a large, limp rag doll and slid off the chair onto the floor. Zapping Hilda's hand with a pointed pinch as she reached for the test tube again, Sabrina walked over and picked up the doll.

"Ow! Hurt!" Rubbing her hand, Hilda scowled at the test tube, then climbed down off her chair and toddled into the living room.

Clad in a miniaturized version of Aunt Zelda's red blouse and pants, the doll had yellow yarn hair stitched into neat curls. The eyes, nose, and mouth were painted onto the flat cloth face. Arms and legs dangled from a solidly stuffed body that emitted a baby-doll cry when pushed.

"Is it even remotely possible you'll be able to work on the antidote now?" Sabrina started as the rag doll's head flopped forward. "Guess not."

Propping the doll on the sideboard out of Hilda's reach, Sabrina went to see what mischief she was getting into in the living room.

Sitting on the floor with a wooden puzzle, Hilda glared at Amanda, who had one of the pieces. "Mine!"

"Don't be so selfish, Hilda," Amanda said. "It isn't nice."

The expert speaks, Sabrina thought wearily. She didn't even want to contemplate the results of a showdown between Quick Draw Hilda and Amanda the Insufferable. "Give it back to her, Amanda, or you *will* be sorry."

"What's she gonna do?" Amanda looked down, sneering. "She can't even talk."

"Just remember I warned you."

"Well, your room is back to normal, Sabrina." Marigold trudged down the stairs. "I think."

Dismayed by what that might mean, Sabrina looked toward Marigold.

"She must have used a dozen different spells—"

"You can have it when I'm done, Hilda!" Amanda snapped.

"Mine!" Hilda pointed.

Amanda disappeared and the puzzle piece fell to the floor.

Picking up the piece, Hilda pounded it into place to finish the puzzle. "All done!"

"That's wonderful." Smiling, Marigold stooped down to look at Hilda intently. "Can you tell me what you did with Amanda? What you wished?"

"Manda go 'way." Hilda held up the puzzle. "Mine!"

"Go away where?" Marigold yanked the puzzle out of Hilda's grasp.

"Mine!"

"Yes, dear, and you can have it back after I find Amanda."

Sabrina saw the glint of displeasure in Hilda's eyes, but once again her reaction time was a split second behind the child's.

" 'Kay." Hilda pointed and Marigold disappeared.

Had Marigold been wished to wherever Amanda was? Sabrina wondered as she watched Hilda replace a puzzle piece that had fallen out of the frame when the puzzle dropped from Marigold's vanishing hands. Since wish magic was only temporary, mother and daughter would pop back in eventually. At the moment, she had more urgent things to worry about.

She was still under the random popping spell.

Salem was a kitten and Aunt Zelda was a rag doll.

Thanks to Hilda, who was a precocious two-and-a-half years old and clueless about the potential consequences of her impulsive wish spells.

And they weren't in the Other Realm where built-in safeguards countered baby magic and mayhem.

Finishing the puzzle again, Hilda smiled at Sabrina. "I did it!"

"Yep. You sure did." Sabrina smiled back, but her mind was reeling.

Hilda's wish magic had worn off the Salem statue within half an hour.

The TV she had wished for had only lasted ten minutes.

Aunt Zelda could change back soon.

Or it could take hours.

Even days, Sabrina realized with a sinking sensation in the pit of her stomach. Nothing could be set right again until Hilda became an adult, but that required the youth potion antidote Aunt Zelda hadn't developed yet.

And there was a lot more at stake than keeping her date with Harvey now.

How much damage could one wish-happy toddler do to the mortal world in a few hours?

Still smiling as Hilda toddled to the couch and opened her backpack, Sabrina decided she really didn't want to find out.

"Mine!" Hilda scowled defiantly when she caught Sabrina watching her.

Sabrina just nodded agreeably. Although her chances of finding the youth potion antidote were slim, she wouldn't have any chance at all if little Hilda made her "go 'way."

☆

Chapter 14

☆

Seven o'clock and all is not well.

Sabrina stared at the computer screen, trying to coordinate Aunt Zelda's notes with the references in her large, leather-bound magic book and the passages she had found in her Handbook.

"'A precise pinch of three-hundred-year-old antelope antler powder neutralizes fermented fern root when not mixed with parsley, sage, rosemary, and thyme.'" Sabrina glanced at the Zelda rag doll perched on the sideboard. "Does that mean not mixed with either parsley, sage, rosemary, or thyme, or all of them together?"

The rag doll sat, limp and unresponsive.

"You're a big help."

Clinging to the rungs under her chair, Salem

batted a string Hilda dangled in front of him. Hilda's incessant giggling was annoying, but preferable to incessant whining, and both tots had stopped pestering her.

"What I need here is a systematic approach." Sabrina chewed the eraser end of a pencil as she scanned her aunt's notes again.

Zelda had concluded that the basic antipotion spell might work if combined with specific measures of certain ingredients used in the youth formula. Isolating the relevant ingredients from the text was a confusing process, however. Taking a flyer, Sabrina pointed and chanted.

"Ingredients on all these pages
List and sort the parts for ages."

"That was pretty lame." Sabrina sighed, then grinned when the computer screen displayed a list of spell components and amounts. "But it worked!"

"Breena." Whining, Hilda tugged on Sabrina's sleeve. " 'Ungry."

"Not now, Hilda. I've almost got this antipotion spell figured out."

" 'Ungry!" Screwing up her face, Hilda began to cry, a wail that began silently and became an ear-piercing crescendo of shrill distress.

Salem jumped into Sabrina's lap and mewed plaintively.

"Breena!"

"All right!" Giving in to the whining child went against Sabrina's grain, but a happy little Hilda was so much safer than an unhappy one. Although almost two hours had passed, Marigold and Amanda hadn't returned, and the rag doll was showing no signs of becoming Aunt Zelda again anytime soon.

With Salem darting ahead and Hilda trailing behind, Sabrina reluctantly left the labtop and went into the kitchen. A quick point filled the cat bowl with kitten chow and minced tuna, which Salem attacked with his normal gusto. "What do you want, Hilda?"

Lip quivering with her subsiding sobs, Hilda shrugged. " 'Ungry."

"Not fussy, huh? This shouldn't be too hard, then." Settling Hilda in the booster seat she had conjured earlier, Sabrina pointed a classic Italian dish Hilda loved with a small Caesar salad on the side.

"Yuck."

"Yuck? Hilda, it's chicken Parmesan with pesto. Your favorite."

"Yuck." Pushing the plate away, Hilda propped her chin in her hands.

"Okay. Let's try this one." Trashing the chicken and replacing it with Rock Cornish game hen stuffed with wild rice, Sabrina looked at Hilda expectantly.

"I don' like it."

Beef bourguignon.

"I don' like it."

Three gourmet choices later, Sabrina threw up her hands in exasperation. "Okay. This is your last chance. You'll either eat this or starve. Got it?"

Pout.

Pointing up a hot dog with chips and a dill pickle, Sabrina was too irritated to appreciate Hilda's cry of delight.

Seven-fifteen.

"I'm going back to the labtop, but I can see you through the door. Just call me when you're done, okay?"

"Gurg."

"And don't talk with your mouth full!"

Giving Hilda a glass of milk, Sabrina dashed back to the dining room. If she was going to get anything accomplished, it would have to be now, while Salem and Hilda were completely engrossed in food. Flatly refusing to take a nap, Hilda was overtired and cranky, which boded no good for anyone within pointing distance of her. Glad that she had warned Harvey she might be late to the roller rink, Sabrina consulted the recipe on the computer and began mixing.

"All done!" Hilda called ten minutes later. "Breena?"

"I'll be there in a second!" Leaning to the side, Sabrina glanced at Hilda, who was licking her finger to pick the potato chip crumbs off her plate. She needed only another minute or two to finish the antidote and decided to risk it. Measuring out the last ingredient, a quarter teaspoon of anti-scorpion venom, she spilled it when Hilda shouted.

"Breena! Wan' down!"

"Coming!" Sabrina hesitated. She could point the child off the booster seat, but she didn't want her running around loose during the delicate final stage of the potion process. Concentrating so her hand would stop shaking, Sabrina carefully scooped again, then scraped off the excess venom powder with a flat edge.

"Breena!" Hilda wailed.

Holding her breath, Sabrina poured the anti-scorpion venom into the beaker. After mixing the venom into the bright red liquid with a long, glass stirrer and filling the dropper, she stood up.

"Breena!" Hilda screamed.

The chair Sabrina had been sitting in suddenly zipped toward the kitchen door, drawn by the powerful force of little Hilda's wrath. Sabrina's heart fluttered. How was she going to get the anti-youth formula potion into Hilda if she was mad enough to wish her into the next county? Or worse?

"Do you want dessert?" Sabrina backed up a step and looked into the kitchen just as Hilda dropped her empty plate on the floor.

Sleeping with his head on the counter, Salem

looked up when the glass dish shattered. He blinked, yawned, and went back to sleep.

" 'Sert?"

"Yeah! 'Sert. I've got something special just for you, but it will take me a minute to fix, okay?"

"Wan' 'sert. Ice cweam."

"Ice cweam! Coming right up." Pointing up a dish of vanilla ice cream with chocolate syrup swirls, Sabrina squeezed the antiyouth formula potion over the top. The ice cream hissed and melted where it touched.

"Here it is!" As Sabrina turned to leave, her gaze swept past the computer screen, then flicked back. A disclaimer light was blinking at the end of the text. Scrolling, she read:

Variations of the basic anti-potion potion may produce side effects.

"Side effects! What side effects?" Sabrina couldn't believe the potion to reverse the youth formula and its side effects produced its own side effects! It was enough to make a witch go organic.

"Ice cweam now!" Hilda banged on the table with her fist, then hurled the half-full glass of milk through the door.

Catching the glass with a point before it smashed against the wall, Sabrina ran into the kitchen. The disclaimer hadn't said *harmful* side effects, and she doubted they could be worse than a toddler witch with wish powers and a temper.

Besides, Aunt Zelda could figure out how to counter any unwanted side effects after she returned to normal.

"Look at this, Hilda!" Sabrina set the dish of potion-spiked ice cream on the table. "Yummy."

"Ice cweam! Sanks, Breena!" Eyes shining, Hilda dug in.

Sitting down to wait for the anti-potion to take effect, Sabrina was again amazed at how quickly she forgave Hilda's monster nature when she was being charming and sweet.

Swallowing the first mouthful, Hilda wrinkled her nose. "Yucky."

Heart flip-flopping, Sabrina tensed. She hadn't stopped to think about how the anti-potion tasted.

"How can ice cream be yucky, Hilda? That's silly. Try it again."

Hilda hesitated, then took another spoonful. Frowning, she swallowed.

Sabrina waited anxiously as Hilda paused again, her spoon suspended over the bowl. How much of the potion did she have to take? That became a moot point when Hilda began eating in earnest. Breathing easier, Sabrina relaxed.

Except nothing happened.

Sabrina frowned as little Hilda held out the empty bowl.

"Mo', peas."

Nothing?

"Mo' ice cweam!" Eyes flashing, Hilda shook the bowl.

"Uh-huh." Dumbfounded, Sabrina reviewed everything she had read and recounted her steps in the measuring and mixing process. Even if she had messed up, *something* should be happening.

"Mo', Breena!"

Suddenly, little Hilda ballooned into giant Hilda.

Mouth agape, Sabrina cringed as Hilda grew to twice her normal size in height and girth. The tiny T-shirt and bunny jumpsuit burst at the seams. Sabrina quickly pointed, dressing Hilda in her "Witchfest '76" T-shirt and gray sweatpants with a size adjustment feature factored in. The plastic booster seat broke into several pieces, and the table resting on her huge knees rose off the floor.

Salem opened one eye, then leaped to his feet, tail fluffed, back arched, hackles raised, and fangs bared.

"Obviously, there's a major glitch in the anti-potion . . ."

Then just as suddenly, Hilda shrank and stopped shrinking when she was her normal adult size. The T-shirt and sweats tightened around her, then loosened again as they adjusted to fit her final form.

Totally wiped out, Sabrina sagged in the chair. "Thank goodness. I've never been so glad to see anyone—"

Scowling at the empty bowl in her hand, Hilda held it out. "Mo' ice cweam, Breena!"

"Uh-oh."

Chapter 15

☆

What am I doing with an empty ice cream bowl in my hand?" Sounding like her usual self, Hilda dropped it. "Did I eat that? I'm on a diet!"

"Aunt Hilda?" Sabrina asked tentatively.

"Yes?" Confused, Hilda eyed her warily. "What?"

"I'll explain later. Right now you've got some serious spell reversing to do." Jumping up, Sabrina grabbed her hand to haul her into the dining room, then released it when her aunt balked. "Sorry. A habit I picked up this afternoon."

Spotting the torn toddler clothes on the floor, Hilda paled. "I'm afraid to ask."

"To make a long story short, Amanda zinged you

with Aunt Zelda's youth potion. By mistake. It was in Marigold's soda, which you drank."

Hilda glanced at baby Salem as he chased a piece of kitten chow across the countertop. "And I became—what?"

"A stinky two-year-old with a temper and a fast finger."

"Enough said. My nanny originated the phrase 'terrible twos' because of me." Sighing, Hilda asked cautiously. "Is the town still standing?"

"Yes, but Marigold and Amanda are missing in action, and Aunt Zelda—" Sabrina winced.

"I'm in big trouble, huh?"

"That depends. Can you reverse the wish-magic spells you made as little Hilda?"

"Yeah, but why would I want to find Amanda and Cousin Marigold any sooner than necessary?" Hilda exhaled shortly. "Wish-magic wears off—eventually."

"Actually, I'm more concerned with Aunt Zelda." Urging her reluctant aunt to follow, Sabrina led the way into the dining room. The rag doll was exactly as she had left it, sitting on the sideboard with drooping arms, legs, and head.

"Okay. Wish her back to normal."

The rag doll remained unchanged.

"Aunt Hilda?" Sabrina looked back as Hilda lifted a test tube of iridescent blue jelly out of the wire rack. "Change Aunt Zelda back, Aunt Hilda."

"Okay, okay." Hilda tossed off a casual point. Holding the test tube up to the light, she seemed mesmerized by the shimmering blue glow.

"I said, 'Don't touch!' " Sliding off the sideboard, Aunt Zelda stormed toward Hilda.

"Mine!" Protectively pressing the test tube against her chest, Hilda dared Zelda to take it away with narrowed eyes and a determined pout.

Aunt Zelda stopped short. "Hilda! You're back."

"Don't touch my tube!"

"I, uh, won't." Zelda looked questioningly at Sabrina. "What's going on here?"

"Well, after Hilda turned you into a rag doll and sent Amanda and Marigold to who-knows-where, I used your research notes to make an anti-potion potion to get Hilda back so she could undo all her spells." Sabrina paused to take a breath. "And there seems to be some baby Hilda left over."

"It scares me to say so, but I understood that." Zelda smiled at Hilda. "You can keep the test tube. At least until I figure out how to compensate for the residual effects."

"Thanks!" Grinning, Hilda sat down on the floor and put a stopper in the tube. "This is such a pretty bottle."

"What about Salem?" Zelda asked.

"He's still a kitten," Sabrina said. "The last time I saw him he was in the kitchen."

"And now he's climbing my back!" Biting her

lip, Zelda gratefully took the mashed fish ball Sabrina quickly conjured and doctored with a dose of the anti-youth formula potion.

Perched on her shoulder, Salem sniffed it, nibbled, then gulped it down in two bites.

"It takes a few minutes to work," Sabrina said. "And it might be a good idea to put him down before it does because—"

Too late! Zelda's knees buckled as Salem ballooned up. Losing his balance, he fell off and made a five-point landing on four paws and a belly. A moment later he shrank to normal size and shook his head.

"Did it work? Do I look younger? Did I grow scales on my ears or anything else equally unbecoming to a cat?"

"Sort of, no, and no," Sabrina said.

"Funny." Salem cocked his head. "I have this overwhelming urge to climb something."

Sabrina quickly moved away from the cat. "Next order of business. Aunt Hilda?"

Chin resting on her folded arms, Hilda stared at the shimmering blue jelly in her test tube.

"Aunt Hilda!"

"What?" Annoyed, Hilda looked up.

Sabrina forced herself to stay calm. "The spell you tried to put on Amanda this morning ricocheted to me! Please, take it off."

"What spell?"

Zelda patiently explained.

"Oh, *that* spell." Rising, Hilda chanted.

"No more random popping into books and TV.
You can come and go here whenever you
please."

Sabrina felt a slight buzzing in her head, then heard a soft *pop.*

"I really am sorry about that, Sabrina." Hilda shrugged. "I had no idea that spell missed Amanda and caught you on the rebound."

"Well, I had an interesting day and no harm done. But if you don't mind, I think I'll test the fix."

"I don't mind." Hilda looked down as Salem dove into the pile of plastic blocks still scattered on the floor. "Cool blocks!"

"Mine!" Salem hissed.

"I think I'd better get busy." Pointing up a fresh cup of tea, Zelda settled in at the labtop.

Dashing into the living room, Sabrina turned on the TV. It was just before eight. A quick flick to change clothes and she could pop to the rink and meet Harvey on time—if she didn't pop into the re-run of *Mission: Impossible* that appeared on the screen.

Martin Landau peeled off a latex mask to the horrified disbelief of the apprehended villain, then got into a black car with the rest of the team and drove away.

But she was still in the living room.

"Yes!" For good measure, Sabrina changed channels and caught the final segment of a local news broadcast.

"Reporting live from Gleason's Toys and Games. Just under an hour ago, chaos erupted in this Devon Street toy store. For reasons the authorities have yet to determine—"

Satisfied her popping problem was over, Sabrina bent down to turn off the TV and froze. Marigold and Amanda, locked in what appeared to be a heated argument, were standing in the curious crowd that had gathered outside the toy store.

"—every battery-operated toy, model, and game turned itself on and went berserk. Ellen Biggs was in the store at the time and is here to give us an eyewitness account."

Focused on Marigold and Amanda, Sabrina saw them vanish from the throng—

"Cars and toy robots were flinging themselves off the shelves and rampaging down the aisles. It's a miracle no one was hurt."

—and heard them when they popped back into the dining room.

"Because," Amanda said defiantly, "after tomorrow I won't be able to have *any* fun."

"That's *not* a good reason, Amanda!" Marigold was only a decibel shy of shouting. "We're going home. Now. Before you cause any more trouble or Hilda decides to send us to Pluto!"

Turning around, Sabrina saw Hilda pick up the remote.

"Thank you, Ms. Biggs. And now back to—"

"—whaddaya mean I got a big nose?" Replacing the newscaster on the screen, a cartoon bulldog was backing a skinny little dog against a fence.

"'Toons!" Clutching the remote, Hilda plopped on the couch and gestured wildly. "Get out of the way, Sabrina!"

Sabrina stepped aside as Marigold hauled Amanda into the foyer and up the stairs.

"I sure hope their linen closet doesn't have any cross-realm traffic delays." Still in her stocking feet, Marigold limped slightly. "The sooner I get you home, the sooner you can apologize to your furniture!"

"I'll never apologize to a bunch of stuffed—*mmmfffm!"*

"Stuff *that!"*

Sabrina laughed aloud as Marigold pointed, muffling Amanda with a rolled-up sock.

"Yeah, I love this part, too, Sabrina." Hilda laughed uproariously as a cartoon fence plank spun around and caught the bully bulldog in the chin.

"I've got a date, Aunt Hilda. Gotta go!"

As she ducked into the front foyer, Sabrina heard the thunder and lightning boom of the linen closet cycling Marigold and Amanda back to the Other

Realm. Quick-changing into a long-sleeved red velour T-shirt and matching slouch socks over black leggings, Sabrina raised her finger to pop herself out—

And the Quizmaster popped in.

"I didn't do it!" Sabrina held up her hand. "On my honor as a permit-carrying witch in training."

"Relax, Sabrina." Wearing a tuxedo with a flashing green bow tie, a sparkling green cummerbund, and twinkling green shoes and carrying a silver-tipped walking stick, the Quizmaster smiled. "I just popped in to let you know I'm giving you an A for your extra-credit project."

"Great!" Sabrina frowned. "What extra-credit project?"

"Making an anti-potion potion that works. Not an easy thing to do. In fact, it's almost impossible for anyone but the super scientific types. Like your Aunt Zelda."

"Really? I did okay, then. Even with the residual side effects."

"What residual side effects?" Leaning on his cane, the Quizmaster arched a quizzical eyebrow.

"Did I say side effects?" Sabrina turned when someone knocked on the front door. "Excuse me. I'd better get that."

The Quizmaster popped over to block the door. "It's not nice to fool the Quizmaster."

"Okay." Sabrina sighed. "There's just a teensy-weensy bit of toddler mentality left in Aunt Hilda."

"That's no problem! Hilda never completely grew up to begin with. What else?"

The visitor knocked again, louder, but Sabrina couldn't see who it was through the Quizmaster. "Salem seems to have retained some of his kitten tendencies, too, but other than that—*nada.*"

"He's a cat. Doesn't count. You're cool. And I've got a date!" Pulling a top hat out of thin air, the Quizmaster bowed, donned the hat, then sang and danced his way out. "'Hey, Venus! Oh, Venus! Make my wish come truuuuue . . .'"

"Weird." Watching the Quizmaster fade out, Sabrina opened the door without looking. "Par for the course around here."

"What is?" A familiar voice asked.

Sabrina whirled. "Mr. Kraft! What are you doing here?"

"I've got a date with Hilda. Is she ready?"

Sabrina hollered over her shoulder, "Aunt Hilda! Mr. Kraft is here!"

"Willard!" Leaping over the back of the sofa, Hilda rushed up smiling, skidded to a halt, then eyed him with a suspicious frown. "Do you like cartoons?"

"Uh—" Mr. Kraft clasped his hands in front of him and leaned forward slightly. "Do you?"

"I asked you first."

Catching the vice-principal's eye, Sabrina emphatically nodded in the affirmative.

"Yes! I love cartoons."

"Good, 'cause tonight we're having pizza delivered and watching a classic-cartoon marathon." Yanking Mr. Kraft by the hand, Hilda hauled him into the living room.

"That sounds like fun. Will we be alone?"

"Sit down, Willard." Hilda pushed Mr. Kraft onto the sofa. "And don't even *think* about touching the remote."

"You're a hard woman, Hilda." Mr. Kraft sighed.

"Pizza?" Salem appeared from parts unknown. "Did someone say pizza? With anchovies?"

Sabrina nodded toward the living room. "Take your best shot, Salem. I think Aunt Hilda's buying."

"Thanks, I will. But first there's something I just gotta do." Crouching and wiggling his haunches, Salem took off toward the bay window, leaped, and climbed the curtains.

Since popping out to the roller rink from the foyer with Mr. Kraft sitting on the sofa wasn't a good idea, Sabrina grabbed her parka off the floor where Hilda had tossed it and started to step outside.

Upstairs, thunder boomed in the linen closet and Cousin Marigold's voice rang down the stairwell.

"A U-turn? When did we make a U-turn? I hope Zelda's got a decent service contract on this closet—"

Closing the front door behind her, Sabrina sighed, glad that everything in the Spellman household was back to normal.

"Weird, but normal." Smiling, she popped out.

About the Author

Diana G. Gallagher lives in Minnesota with her husband, Marty Burke, three dogs, three cats, a cranky parrot, and a guinea pig called Red Alert. When she's not writing, she spends her time walking the dogs, puttering in the yard, playing the guitar, and going to garage sales looking for cool stuff for her grandsons, Jonathan, Alan, and Joseph.

A Hugo Award–winning artist, Diana is best known for her series *Woof: The House Dragon.* Dedicated to the development of the solar system's resources, she has contributed to this effort by writing and recording songs that promote and encourage humanity's movement into space. She also loves Irish and folk music and performs at local coffeehouses and science fiction conventions around the country.

Her first adult novel, *The Alien Dark,* appeared in 1990. She and Marty coauthored *The Chance Factor,* a STARFLEET ACADEMY VOYAGER book. In addition to other STAR TREK novels for intermediate readers, Diana has written many books in other series published by Minstrel Books, including *The Secret World of Alex Mack, Are You Afraid of the Dark,* and *The Mystery Files of Shelby Woo.* She is currently working on original young adult novels for the Archway Paperback series *Sabrina, the Teenage Witch.*